HOUSE CALL

AND OTHER STORIES

For my dear friends,
Frankie and Ben

Dan

by

Daniel C. Bryant

Several of these stories have previously appeared as follows:

The Return, *Nimrod International Journal*
Atlantis, Balzac, En Route, *Sixfold*
Home Free, *Bellevue Literary Review*
House Call, *Madison Review*
Armistice Day, *Crab Orchard Review*

ISBN: 978 16311 10 122

Cover design by Dale K. Bryant and Ndigal Fall.

Printed in the United States of America.

For Dale

CONTENTS

ATLANTIS

"German short-haired pointer."

Murray turned to Cal.

"Used to have one," Cal went on. "Or Greta did. She hunted, you know. Greta."

They were reclining in parallel lounge chairs on the deck of Murray's parents' cottage. It was early evening, a breeze beginning to roughen the lake out by Atlantis, the tiny island his mother—"the professor"—had so named. Closer in, near where they'd been swimming, the dog's head just broke the surface.

"You getting cold?" Murray asked.

"You don't care about the dog?"

"I don't care about the wife."

Murray stood, picked up their empties, and went inside. In the bedroom he hoisted his duffel up onto the unmade bed and groped through it until he came to his flannel shirt. He watched himself in the bureau mirror, pulling the shirt on and buttoning the lower buttons, adjusting the collar, then combing his fingers through his still-wet hair. His parents' mirror, this was, rough-framed, reflector of who knows what all those summers ago.

On his way back outside he stopped to pull Cal's windbreaker from the clothes littering the living room floor.

"Her name was David," Cal said as Murray sat back down.

"*Her* name?"

"The bitch's. Greta's sense of humor."

The dog, the apex now of a long V in smoother water, was nearing the shore. His quick coughs broke the silence and as he got closer they could see he had something—a ball, it

1

looked like—in his mouth. Someone must have thrown it for him, probably from the dock of the cottage next door.

"Sure you're not cold?" Murray stroked the back of Cal's forearm and offered the jacket. "You're all goose bumpy."

"Cutis anserina."

"Cutest what?"

"Anserina. What we call them in medicine. Little erections, actually. Hair hard-ons. From back when we all had fur."

"Cool."

Almost a year, now, they'd known each other, since that autumn afternoon when Cal had wandered into Murray's furniture-making shop, and still Murray didn't know how to take those medicalisms of his. Were they information? Boasts? Both? He couldn't imagine springing a "miter joint" or a "spline" on Cal when Cal commented on one of his pieces. But maybe that was the way it was to be with them, the roles relationships like theirs implied.

"You know those people?" Cal asked.

"Those people."

"Yeah. Next door."

Murray looked through the trees to where Cal finally pointed, but didn't see anyone at first. "Millers, must be. George and Rose. Had that cottage forever. Way before us anyway."

"They know? About you?"

"How would they? My folks don't even know."

"'Cause *you* know, sweetheart. That's how people know."

What a very Cal sort of thing to say. A doctor, an intensivist he called himself, who handled the sickest hospital patients, Cal had learned to reduce that desperate world to residual truths, no matter the consequences. He's brain dead and, sorry, but we can't fix that. Guess I'm gay, Greta, and, sorry, but I'm outta here. With woodworking, on the other hand, there was just the wood.

"There he goes again."

Murray looked: the dog, snout held high, was paddling back out past the canoe tied to the end of the Millers' dock.

2

And this time, through the trees, Murray could see by the diving board the one who must have thrown the ball—Kevin, the middle Miller. He was wearing yacht-club white pants and a striped shirt. And sitting on the board beside him, tan legs crossed, holding up a wine glass as if toasting the view, a young woman.

Fantasy fit for his mother, this was—man and woman on dock, setting sun, iconic calls of loons. Monogamous, those loons, she would explain in anthropology-speak. For life. Their first summer at the lake, when he was thirteen, she had packed picnic lunches for him and Sherrie, Kevin's sister, to take to Atlantis. She had driven them the twelve miles to the movies in town, given them extra money, extra time, for sodas and talk afterward. Yet he'd often suspected that that fantasy might have been why—in the paradoxical way of fantasies— he'd wandered down to the Millers' dock one night when Sherrie had turned in early. Might have been why, without a word, he had lain down next to Kevin on the smooth, still-warm planks. Might have been why he had stayed there pretending to watch for shooting stars, all the while thrilling to the close heat of a body so safely, so deliciously like his own. Why, finally, and most fantastically, he had reached for Kevin's hand and triggered the punch that ended all contact with the Millers. The punch that still burned his cheek whenever the memory resurfaced.

"Going after those two loons," Cal was saying.

"Where?" Murray pushed his glasses in tighter, the memory away.

"Those are loons, aren't they? By that little island? Divers, the Brits call them."

Hard as he tried, Murray couldn't make out anything, but he had no doubt they were there. He had seen and heard loons on the lake every summer he'd come, and he and Cal had heard their mournful warble the previous night. Not, Cal had said, a commentary on their love-making, he hoped.

"Better not be loons," Cal added. In a moment he stood. "Actually, I do feel a bit of coolth coming on."

They headed back inside, into the bathroom, and pulled

3

off their trunks. Murray could see that, thanks no doubt to the chill, Cal wasn't stiff at all. That was a relief: he was still sore from last night, and anyway he wasn't finished with the loons.

"Better not be?"

"Yeah. For the dog's sake. Say, you look good in skin. Anybody ever tell you that?"

"Let me get us some towels."

When Murray returned, Cal was standing at the toilet. He shook off the last drops and flushed. The water pump rumbled behind the wall.

"Pointers aren't sheepdogs," Cal said, stepping into the shower stall and pulling the plastic curtain behind him. "They're bird dogs. Gun dogs. But they're still bred to focus. We were in England this time? Lake District?"

His words were lost in the sudden drum of water against the metal sides of the stall. This rustic shower was nowhere near as civilized as the big, Italian marble one in Cal's condo. There they could bathe together easily, talking and laughing in the billowing steam as they lathered each other with Cal's exotic soaps.

Minutes later Cal stepped out, his black hair pasted to his high forehead, water coursing down his torso, down his long legs and now slightly swollen member to pool on the linoleum. Murray handed him a towel and stepped into the stall himself. He washed quickly, expecting the curtain to be snapped back any minute.

"So you were in England...," he said as he began to dry off.

"With Greta. Last time we slept together. One of our better fucks, actually. Anyway, that part of England is wall-to-wall sheep. More sheep than rocks. Ever been there?"

"Never. Never left Orono 'til I was nine. When we moved down to Portland."

"Well, let me tell you, they're everywhere. And it's sheepdogs look after them. Amazing animals. Heat-seek right onto 'em. They say you're driving and you see a sheepdog crouched in a field you better stop quick, 'cause that dog might smash right into the car he's so focused on his sheep.

4

Right into it. Bam! Like that."

Murray flinched at the smack of Cal's fist in his palm. "Impressive," he said, his cheek already burning.

They walked into the bedroom, straightened the bed-clothes, and began dressing.

"Love that cedar attar," Cal said, tipping his head back and sniffing loudly. "But my point is—no pun intended—pointers aren't crazy as sheepdogs. Ours wasn't anyway. Got run over, but not her fault. That I know of."

"Sorry, Cal."

"Yeah. Shitty. 'Bout killed Greta. So, town for pizza before the main event?"

"Sounds good," Murray said, though it didn't, not just yet anyway.

When they walked back outside, the sky had gone indigo and starry. A crescent moon tilted low above the black saw tooth of the Canadian shore. Next door, lights flickered through the intervening leaves and the throb of a musical bass could just be heard. The dock was empty.

Cal strode across the yard toward the car. Murray held back, then walked to the far edge of the deck. He looked out across the lake. Even though it was a Saturday, there was no sign of life anywhere—no boats, no jet skies. Not even any lights on the Canadian side. It was a timeless northern Maine evening like the ones he'd spent there all those years ago: mother with a pile of galleys to edit, father with his flies and his Scotch, sister sequestered with her Harlequins. And he, whittling a chain out of driftwood, trying to remember, as link broke free from link, just what exactly had happened there on the Millers' dock that night.

A splash, ripples, a silver V.

"Cal!"

"What?"

"C'm'ere a minute."

The car door slammed. He heard the slap of sandals on the deck, smelt soap as Cal leaned in close to look where Murray was pointing.

"Oh yeah. Him, all right. You got a 'scope or anything?"

Murray ran back into the living room. In the wicker basket by the chimney, among the board games, the lures and batteries and paperbacks, he found his mother's old opera glasses.

"This is all we've got," he said, back on the deck.

Cal worked the focus wheel as he scanned back and forth. "Oh, there they are! Way the hell out."

Murray took the binoculars, but he couldn't seem to orient himself until he took off his own glasses and pressed the eyepieces in close. There, beyond the silhouette of Atlantis, he finally saw them, two loons, their necks black quotation marks against the dark water.

He put his glasses back on. "The dog after them?"

"Nothing else out there."

"What should we do?"

"Get pizza. Get laid. C'mon."

"He can't swim all that way, Cal. And back."

"He'll turn around. Or there's that island. What'd your mom call it?"

"I thought you were worried about the dog."

Cal held out his keys and jingled them. Murray turned and saw the V's arms lengthen and glisten as the dog moved steadily away.

"You're so worried," Cal said, "go next door. Their dog, right?"

But Murray already had his sandals off, his shorts.

The water, when he hit it, was colder than before. It stopped his breath, but he fought his way forward until with a gasp he fell into a rhythmic, splashless crawl. With each lift of his right arm, each suck of air, he strained to see Atlantis' skyline.

It was his mother who had taught him to swim, breathe out under water so he'd be ready for the next intake of air— Don't panic!—when he turned his head to the side. His mother who, once they started coming to the cottage, had made him do laps back and forth between two birch tree markers before he settled down on the dock to sunbathe or whittle or read. She'd said comfort in the water could save his life some day, the way it had hers that time in the Indian Ocean. Another of

6

easy breath, another descent. Y camp. Skinny dipping. That slow bob up and down, warm, silky water caressing you everywhere. You could do it for hours. Up and down. Up and down. All those summer buddies. The pleasure of survival. The survival of pleasure. Though what did he know, back then, of either? What did they?

But the dog. Treading again he revolved slowly, blinked and spat. The shadow of Atlantis was there but out of place, moved somewhere behind him now when he wasn't paying attention. That's what she'd said: it moved, or sank. Disappeared into the depths of its own myth. Or, no, he'd swum past it, set a record he'd never sought or now she'd ever know.

In the distance a warble, an echo shivering in the air the way he now shivered in the water. Still just as far away. Were the loons alarmed, keeping their distance, luring like sirens?

He dog-paddled. Another splash in the face. Down and up again. But with each drop his legs reached deeper into the cold; his arms grew flimsier. The disgust of slime, of scales and claws.

Fathom! That was the word, the word his father had used: I can't fathom it, Murray. I just can't fathom it. He had to rise. He had to have air, wherever that was. Handfuls and armloads of water and then finally lungfuls of pure darkness. He gasped and lunged, dragging the entire lake upward and forward, until, stumbling, he fell hard.

The tiny island had no real beach. When he and Sherrie had canoed there it was always a challenge to find a proper place to eat, some boulder, some broad tree root where they could sit, bare feet in the water, basket between them, and dole out the sandwiches, the chips and drinks, cookies and fruit, his mother had so carefully prepared. This time, though, solid ground was proper enough. As his head cleared, he crawled from the rocky water's edge to a mossy rise, curled and hugged his shaking. His breathing slowed.

"Doggie," he whispered hoarsely, as if he shouldn't be overheard. Silence, but for the sense of distant music, of lapping. He sat up, then stood. He called louder, slapping his thigh, "Here, boy. C'mon. Good boy."

8

As if in answer, a faraway call. Cal? Should be Cal, but he wasn't ready to answer. Not yet. He was still listening. No rustle of branches, no panting, no tinkle of tags. The dog was still out there somewhere, driven, oblivious. No point in trying to find him again. That's the way of nature, what Cal would say anyway. The image of the dog's watery suffering and death would fade as all memories do.

He sat back down. Music, still, and light from the Millers', must be. A little more rest, and he might try to swim back. He didn't need Cal now. Just a branch, driftwood.

Not all memories do fade, though. Not that of Kevin's heat on that long ago dock. Of his fist. Sherrie's two-word note the next day—"I understand." His fear of talking to her again because what if she did while he didn't? Marcia, Lisa in the back seat of his mother's convertible, Will and Lance in the locker room, college lasting six months because there was only one subject he cared about and no professors, no courses, for that. No, not those memories. Their kind don't fade. They mustn't. What would be left of us if they did?

"Murray!" Cal's voice all right, closer, and closer to anger this time: "Murray!"

"Over here! The end!" He waved his arms over his head.

Dark motion on the water, becoming shapes.

"Jesus, man, we been looking all over." Cal dragged the prow of a canoe up into the undergrowth. He grabbed Murray by the arm, then whipped off his jacket and wrapped it around Murray's shoulders, embracing him in warmth.

"You were after the dog, Murr?"

Murray looked past Cal toward the voice. Whiteness glowed in the stern of the canoe: Kevin's trousers.

"Yeah. Yeah. The dog."

"Shoulda come over," Kevin went on. "Like your friend here. Take the canoe. You could've...."

"Yeah," Murray said again. "Guess so. You get him?"

"Who?" Cal asked.

"The dog. You get the dog?"

"Oh, he came back," Kevin answered. "He always does."

"They're good swimmers, those pointers."

9

"Yeah, Cal, so you said." Murray pulled the jacket tighter around himself, waded over to the canoe and stepped in. It lurched at his weight, dropping him quickly onto the ribs.

Cal pushed off until the scraping stopped, climbed into the bow and started paddling. "Get you back to the cottage," he called out. "Warmed up. You're hypothermic, you know."

"Right," Murray said. "Hypothermic. Get you every time."

"Say," Kevin said from behind him, "why don't you guys come over for a drink? My sister Sherrie and a couple friends are up and...."

"Alcohol's not such a good idea when...."

"Sure, Kevin," Murray interrupted. "Could use a drink."

The two men paddled in silent unison, the canoe thrusting forward with each stroke. Beyond the curve of Cal's back and the rhythm of his powerful arms, Murray could just distinguish the dark suggestion of shoreline, blurred light. How close they already seemed.

"By the way," Kevin called out behind him, "I'm Kevin. Kevin Miller. My folks' place, where we're staying."

"Cal," Cal answered over his shoulder, not breaking rhythm. "Cal Peebles."

Murray turned. "Cal used to be my lover, Kevin. How you guys been, anyway?"

10

BALZAC

Ask me back then about intermediary metabolism, the Circle of Willis, the seven causes of amyloidosis, and I can quote you chapter and verse. But Tonkin? Warhol? Dylan? Pot? The Beats? Aware, almost ashamed, of the narrowness of my pre-med education, most Saturday mornings after Clinical Pathology Conference I hang up my white jacket, shelve my books, and head for the subway. If any place has culture, it's got to be Manhattan. It certainly wasn't, or if it was I missed it, Massillon, Ohio.

Occasionally on these outings I visit The Museum of Modern Art in midtown, and this one Saturday afternoon the fall of second year, I'm sitting on a bench in the museum's Sculpture Garden. It's pleasantly warm and I'm happy to rest up after miles of galleries. For a while I simply admire *Balzac* looming mightily in the distance, but gradually my eyes wander to a young woman sitting on a nearby bench. By shifting my weight and cocking my head, as if studying Rodin's treatment of the great writer, I can study her as well. She's wearing a flowered dress and sandals and has frizzy hair that glows like a brown halo in the reflected sunlight. When occasionally she looks up at a passerby, I can better make out her features—large, dark eyes, even as she squints; an indoor pallor that, along with defined cheekbones, gives her a hungry, oddly appealing look; and a prominent nose, slightly hooked. Aquiline, I think writers call it.

And that's the thing: she's not all that attractive, and yet she attracts me. Maybe it's because I haven't had a girlfriend to speak of since junior year at Williams. Maybe it's because she looks such an authentic part of the New York scene. Maybe it's because she's alone, vulnerable, writing secrets in a spiral notebook, smiling to herself off and on as she does.

11

Whatever the reason, when she finally closes her notebook, stands, and walks back into the museum, I get up and follow her.

She crosses the lobby and disappears through a doorway—STAFF ONLY.

It's mid-afternoon; she works there with art, has been on her break, and is writing the great American novel. Perfect. I sit down on the marble floor and lean back against the wall to consider my options. One is to enter the forbidden world of STAFF ONLY, the sort of thing I don't normally do. One is to go back upstairs and give *Guernica* another look. Another is to move on to the Frick or Guggenheim, or continue on down to the Village to a coffee house where I've seen people protesting things. Heading back uptown to the dorm is not an option. Yet.

I buy a booklet about Klimt in the museum shop, return to my station, and begin leafing through the glossy pages.

Just before five she appears. She walks right past, giving wide berth to my outstretched legs, and smiling ever so slightly, just the way she had earlier in the garden. I get up and follow her out to the sidewalk. She stops and turns.

"He wore that when he wrote," she says.

I look back over my shoulder, but it's me she's talking to.

"His dressing gown. Or maybe you knew that."

"No, I didn't."

"Not that it matters."

"No, no. It matters. That he did. Or I didn't."

She'd noticed me earlier. I go on, "He's so grand. Like his name. Balzac. I wonder if he'd look so grand if his name was, I don't know, mine. Curtis."

"Yes! Yes!" She nods vigorously, laughing. "You're right. BALZAC!" She looks up, squinting at the name exploding above us. "Wow!"

Never before—or in the forty years of patients, colleagues, neighbors, family since—has an offhand comment of mine made such an impression on a person. And this isn't just any person. This is a New York person. A museum person.

"Well," she says, her face back to baseline, "I've got to

meet someone."

"Oh. Right. See you. Or not."

She turns and walks away down 53rd Street—biggish hips, slightly pigeon-toed, but a smart, directed walk—and soon I lose the flowered dress in the palette of the midtown crowd.

I head north, replaying our conversation. People frown and veer away when I mouth BALZAC, but I don't care. I said something important. I made an impression. I was funny in New York. I can see her laugh, hear her "Yes! Yes!", her "Wow!" And what's more, I have to see and hear it all again. By the time I think subway, I'm almost to Harlem.

Second year in medical school, at least back in the Sixties, was all pre-clinical stuff—pathology, physiology, pharmacology. The only patients we saw were the ones rolled into the amphitheaters on gurneys and exhibited for their deformities and gaits, their tremors and murmurs; we had yet to engage a patient one-on-one. In preparation for that great day, I do my best to keep up with my studies, but it's even harder now. Instead of cirrhosis, endocarditis, nephritis, I'm thinking MoMA, flowered dress, "Yes! Yes!" Harvey, my dorm neighbor, and study partner, says I'm dragging him down.

The next Saturday afternoon, book in hand this time, I'm back with Balzac. When she arrives, in blouse and long skirt, I get up and stroll around the courtyard, delaying once to inspect Picasso's *She Goat*. Finally I arrive at her bench.

"Hello again," I say.

She looks up, shading her eyes. "Again?"

"Oh, right. That would be next time. If there is one."

She doesn't invite me to sit down, but after a moment I do.

"Tragic," she says, pointing to *The Rebel*, which I've positioned face up on my lap.

"It is, pretty."

"His dying."

"Oh, that." At the time I didn't know that Camus had died in an auto accident four years before. "Yes. Very tragic."

We sit there regarding Balzac's vast dark planes, vora-

13

cious eyes.

"You work here?" I ask.

"I do."

"As?"

"Cataloguer."

"You log cattle."

"Yes! Yes!" she says, laughing and nodding her head. Her frizzy hair bounces; my heart leaps. "Somebody's got to."

"Even on Saturdays."

"Never on Sunday. And you?"

I'm in. I tell her about medical school and she asks if we call a cadaver him or her, or it, and where the mind might be. She even asks me to look at a lump that's been bothering her. I take the ink-stained finger she holds out and gently palpate the swelling. Heberden's node, I tell her. Inflammation of the distal interphalangeal joint. Nothing to worry about. Tylenol if it bothers.

She nods. I don't let go.

She agrees to dinner.

I'm in love for sure. I tell Harvey. He tells me studies show Second Year is the worst year to fall in love. What about the Tropical Medicine practical just four days off? If he gets 92 or less, he's firing me.

Hannah—that's her name—picks an Italian restaurant in the East Village, near where she lives, for that first dinner; and the next weekend invites me for stir-fry at her apartment. Soon we're spending Sundays together, reading Ginsberg on the Staten Island Ferry, critiquing walkers in Central Park, listening to baroque music up at the Cloisters. We tell each other our birthdays, former pets' names, worst movies, first memories. Early December, two months after meeting, we climb into bed.

It's a memorable night, all right, though not in the way I was expecting. Almost halfway to being a doctor, with all that implies anatomically and physiologically, not to mention authoritatively, I'm still inexperienced as Adam. I do know about condoms, and have been prepared for a couple of weeks already, but my sexual debut there in that street-lit room on that squeaky single bed is as awkward as it is fast. I immediately collapse into a deep sleep from which I waken periodically to a mixture of delicious satisfaction and dawning apprehension.

Pressed up against her from behind, my right arm draped over her torso and hand cupping her left breast, I have become aware of her heartbeat. From Anatomy and Physical Diagnosis, I know that the cardiac Point of Maximum Intensity lies immediately below the left breast, in the fifth intercostal space, mid-clavicular line. It's where the apex of the heart abuts the chest wall, and where the left ventricular systoles can be easily palpated between the ribs. Where one can all but touch another's heart.

Only thing is, the rhythmic tap of this heart against the side of my hand is not entirely regular. Every few beats a pause or skip seems to occur. Is this some post-coital delusion of mine, or have I stumbled on my first cardiac pathology? I try to improve my finger position.

Perhaps put off, Hannah removes my hand from her chest and works herself onto her back. She offers me a joint, which I've never tried before, and which I decline, not wanting to confuse the situation further. We lie there in parallel as I listen to her breathing. It seems regular enough, easy. I try to get a glimpse of her neck veins, which I have recently learned become distended in cases of right heart failure, but the light and the angle are not in my favor.

We make love again. She says it's better for her this time. Not "Yes! Yes!" better, but better enough. I'm happy. She lights up. I sleep.

All through Christmas vacation back home in Massillon I think about Hannah. I think about wandering the Village with her, about the hours in the automats sharing cheesecake and coffee while I tell her what I'm learning and she tells me what she's writing, about seeing *The Fantasticks* off Broadway and singing "deep in December it's nice to remember" all the way back to the apartment. I tell my folks, yes, I've met a girl and

15

yes, she's pretty. Well, pretty pretty. Smart as all get out. Dropped out of Bennington to become a cataloguer. At this really famous museum. And she's going to become a writer. Is one I guess. Do I love her? Well, I really like her, that's for sure. Be careful, they say—it is New York.

When I take the bus in from JFK I go directly to Hannah's. It's a quick strip, passionate reunion, and the night is much too short. In the morning before I head uptown, I take her wrist as if to check on her Heberden's node. Same pulse.

In the medical library over the next few days I pore through cardiology textbooks. The arrhythmia sections, though, are way over my head, filled with obscure electrophysiology and cardiograms and allusions to conditions I can't even pronounce. Again Harvey threatens to fire me, and when I finally tell him what's bothering me, he says, "Bail, man. Before it's too late."

It's cold now in the winter city, stinging winds howling through the cross-town canyons. We have to stay inside— diners, museums, her apartment. She reads me stories she's writing, and tells me how original my comments are. "Yes! Yes!" she exclaims, delighting me with her delight.

But is she unwell? As I watch her curled on her bed, sheaf of typewritten papers in her hand, I can't help wondering. Any minute might she slump unconscious, victim of a lethal progression of the arrhythmia I've detected? Should I say something to her about it? Ask her, casually, if she's ever been told....

Of course, maybe—probably is more like it—it's nothing. Back in my room I take my own pulse, vicariously hers. A periodic slowing, it seems now. Maybe I'm overreacting. Maybe I'm suffering from a version of medical student syndrome, that insidious condition in which one comes to regard the ordinary as ominous. I decide that to mention my concern to Hannah will only create unnecessary anxiety.

I do call Dr. Winslow Parker's office, though. Dr. Parker is one of the cardiologists on Presbyterian's staff, as well as one of our more approachable physical diagnosis instructors.

16

Over the phone I present the case the way I've heard upper-classmen do it at grand rounds: This is a twenty two year old white single MoMA cataloguer, with no known cardiac history.... But it's clear within minutes that Dr. Parker would need to actually see Hannah before offering any advice, though he doesn't sound all that concerned. Sinus arrhythmia most likely, he says—pulse variation with the respiratory cycle, more common in females. "Bring her into the office to make sure. Happy to take a look at her for you."

For you? For me? Have I then assumed responsibility for Hannah? Would "bringing her into the office" seal that? Has sleeping with her these past three months so committed me to her that I must spend the rest of my life—her life, at least—tending to a potential cardiac cripple? Would she see it that way?

Things aren't quite the same between us after this. It feels like I've lost another kind of virginity, and a more significant one at that. After reading up on sinus arrhythmia, I work more questions into our conversations. My mother said once I'd been a "blue baby." Had she been one by any chance? Did she ever have pains in joints other than that Heberden one, "growing pains," rheumatic fever or anything? I sometimes get faint in the heat. Of course it's cold now, but did she ever? Faint? Just wondering. Oh, and your family, they're so interesting, Eastern Europe and all. Any of them, I don't know, die young?

I watch her as we climb the three flights to her apartment, looking for evidence of dyspnea on exertion. At bedtime, in the guise of foreplay I check her ankles for edema. I even watch her during sex, though without, I'm sure, the requisite objectivity.

The worst part of my new attitude, though, is that my suspicion of one imperfection has sensitized me to others. Her nose, for instance. It's not particularly attractive. I've known that from the beginning, preferring to think of it as classical, Mediterranean. Her hips are definitely on the wide side, her

17

hair not really as appealing as the long blonde locks of the girls I'd noticed growing up in the heartland. The joy that I've had being with her, sharing her humor and zest for life and for stories, reveling in her Yes! Yes!, all gradually recedes into clinical appraisal. Have I, I wonder, ever truly loved her? Is it just being loved I've loved? And if I haven't truly loved her, does that let me off the hook? Does it permit me to take Harvey's counsel and bail?

It's not fair to exclude her from my dilemma, of course. Whether I have truly loved her or not, I've certainly given her reason to think I do. She loves me, or at least has said so. But does she? Is it my being a medical student, with such a guaranteed future, rather than just the insightful, appealing person she's made me think I am, that has attracted her? Am I her ticket out of the world of catalogues and one-room walkup apartments?

Harvey cans me. I've gone from bad to worse, as far as he's concerned. Studying alone now, watching my grades drop, I realize that my involvement with Hannah is threatening my medical future, not to mention my parents' expectations. That alone is reason to break things off. I compose a letter in which I explain my difficulty keeping up with my studies while thinking of her, and my decision, in spite of it breaking my heart, to end our relationship. At least for a while. And speaking of hearts, I add, I thought I'd noticed once a little skip of yours. It's probably nothing but you might want to ask your doctor about it.

I take the subway downtown, walk across to the East Side, climb the stairs, and quietly slip the letter under her door.

Toward the end of my senior year, returning from the clinic one afternoon I find in my mailbox a small, flat package addressed in a familiar hand. "Dear Curtis," the enclosed letter begins,

> Please consider this note an effort, not to
> get you back, but only to wish you all success
> as you embark, as you must be about to, on

18

your medical career. I hope you are well. Balzac and I are, and thought you might like to see this issue of *Wesley Review.* It contains "One too many mornings," which you may remember helping me revise once upon a time.

Fondly, Hannah

Reasonably computer-savvy now in my retirement, I often pass the time browsing the Internet, looking up information about the Sixties, say, that famous decade I took so for granted even as I lived it. Sometimes I think of googling Hannah Hershon. Would that still be her name? Might she be the author of other stories, novels perhaps? Might I be in one, the I I was then, or that she saw? I have kept the letter and literary magazine she sent me. Every once in a while I take them out and read them, though I've never shown them to any one else, including either of my former wives or any of my children. The story is quite a good one, about a couple lost in a city, and her letter tells me, I think, that there was never anything really wrong with her heart. Only with mine.

EN ROUTE

The vinyl burned the backs of Arlie's legs. She cranked down her window. Vern ooh'ed and ee'ed as he worked himself in behind the wheel: he felt it, too.

"Seatbelt, Vern." With grand gestures she fastened her own, and from the clicks and groans beside her, knew that Vern was trying to secure his, one of those many little rituals, like holding hands, or running the water cold, that her husband —her physical husband at least—could still carry out about as well as ever. When he finally grew quiet, she felt for the upper left button on her watch: "Two-Thirteen-P-M".

"Plenty of time," she said, as if in reply, and then, "Roll down your window, Vern. Get us some air in here." She opened the purse on her lap and felt for the keys. Once she had isolated the car key—bigger than either the apartment or locker one, toothed on both sides—she held it up and jangled the bunch in Vern's direction.

"Got it? That's it. Put it in your keyhole there and turn. Like we do." She pointed to the left, the general direction of the steering column, and heard the metallic tap and scratch of the key finding its way into—she hoped—the ignition switch.

"You turning? You've got to turn it, Vern, like this," and she made a little pinching twist with the fingers of her right hand.

Nothing happened. She felt a bead of sweat tickle between her breasts. She reached across the console until she brushed Vern's arm, then followed it out to his hand: he was holding the key all right, but up by the dashboard, near the radio. TV repairman so many years, he'd never forget about knobs and dials.

"Vern!" she shouted, slapping his hand. "We're starting the car, for God's sake! The key! Then do the foot. You

21

know!"

Clinks followed, and in another moment the old Buick's engine revved three times like a hotrod at a light, then settled into a muttering idle. Throatier than last week, that was for sure: next thing would be a new muffler.

This driving routine of Vern and Arlie's was one they'd been following for almost two years now, ever since Arlie's macular had become so bad that she couldn't get her license renewed. And though Vern's memory meant he couldn't find his way around town any more, his vision seemed fine, and his old driving reflexes had stayed in his limbs just as surely as Arlie's old itineraries had stayed in her imagination. Between the two of them, they could get just about anyplace they had to.

Today, anyplace they had to was Vern's neurologist, then the Shop 'n' Save for a rotisserie chicken.

"Any cars coming on your side?" Arlie asked. "You looking to see? Pay attention now."

They'd stopped soon after Vern had pulled out of the parking place. From that timing, and the sticky whine of tires on pavement, Arlie knew they'd reached the exit to the elderly-housing lot.

"You looking to see?" she repeated, louder.

"Yes."

"You tell me, now, when there's a good long space." And a few seconds later, "How about now, Vern? Look out your window. Still cars?"

"No cars."

"Pull out! Quick now, Vern. To the right." She swept her hand widely, knuckling glass. Tires squealed, her neck snapped.

No horns, no crash, just a cool cheek from moving air. She opened her eyes on lesser darkness, and drew her legs back in.

It had been a month since their last visit to Dr. Drummond, the one who had started Vern on the experimental drug for his memory. In fact, Arlie was quick to tell anyone who would listen, Vern was enrolled in a nationwide study, run by specialists down in Boston, which meant free medicine, free brain scans and blood tests, free appointments. They'd both had to sign consents—which she couldn't read anymore than he could grasp—indicating they knew the drug should do some good, though might also do some harm; and for four months now, at seven-thirty sharp every morning, Arlie had been making him swallow his two big capsules with a full glass of water. So far, she hadn't seen much change.

"Have we gotten to the light yet, Vern?"

"No."

"When we do, go right again." As she pointed, she felt the car slowing, then smoothly stopping. It was cooler here, and dimmer: the shadow of the Stanley Building, it must be. Yes, the dry cleaner smell, from next door.

"Light red?"

"Yes. Red."

"When it's green, go right." She pointed again. "Wait for green now, the one on the bottom. You watching?"

This wasn't the shortest way to Dr. Drummond's office, Arlie knew, but this time of day it would mean the fewest cars, the fewest delivery vans, the least chance of an accident. There would be stop signs—three of them all told—but Vern was good with stop signs. Better, really, than she'd ever been in her own days behind the wheel.

"At the stop sign after next we're going to go left." Shortly, they stopped, but soon after starting up again, slowed.

"What is it, Vern?" Arlie asked. "Something in the road? Something in the way?" He shouldn't be braking just yet: this should be the long block. She swung her head back and forth, hoping for a shard of peripheral vision. Nothing, and with a jerk that set her seatbelt, the car stopped dead.

"Vern, what are you doing?" They couldn't be much farther than the Pizza Hut. "Answer me!"

"My son."

"Your what was that, Vern?" Malcolm had died thirty-three years ago, triggering a tripwire on night patrol, the official letter had said. Forgetting all about that had been the one saving grace of Vern's dementia. Would that blindness had

23

done the same for her.

"Vern...." But the car door behind her squeaked open. Rustling sounds, a grunt. Slam.

"Drive, gramps! Got a gun under this camo."

Arlie shrank, her heart wild under the chest strap. Perfume in the air. She reached for Vern's arm.

"You deaf? I said, Drive!"

"What... what is this?" Arlie asked straight ahead. "Who...?"

"C'mon! Get a move on!"

Arlie leaned toward her husband. "Any cars coming, Vern?"

"No cars. Coming."

"Go ahead, then, down the road. To the stop sign. Like we do." As the breeze from her window resumed, something knocked Arlie's left arm, tore her purse from her lap.

"What's your bank?" The raspy voice was a young man's. Young smoker's.

"Bank of America," Arlie said.

"Where we're goin' then!"

In another minute, the car came to a stop. Must be the intersection now. That program once about holdups—what never to do. Police stations. She tried to line up streets. On account of the crowds at the Farmer's Market, there should be a policeman at Monument Square. But how.... Was this really Tuesday? Were they really...?

"I said, Drive! You stupid or something?"

"Ray." It was a girl's voice directly behind Arlie, syrupy, verging on whiney: the voice of the perfume.

"Shut up!"

"Keep straight, Vern. If nothing's coming. Going to be all right. Everything's going to be all right."

"What's with the geezer?"

"He needs help with directions. Sometimes. He... he doesn't remember so well."

"You drive, then. Pull over!"

"I can't."

"What? Drive?"

24

"See."

"Oh, shit! Shit, shit, shit!"

"Go left here, Vern." And then, emboldened by the strange new advantage her blindness seemed to be giving her, Arlie finally turned her head toward the voices. "May I ask what this...? Why we're going...?"

"May I ask, Shut the fuck up, lady!"

$2016 in the savings account. Arlie knew the amount, including this month's interest, to the dollar. Both of their Social Security direct deposits not due until Wednesday. The CDs... they wouldn't have to know about that part. But it wasn't the money that was the worry: they had her MasterCard now, address, both their Medicare numbers. Identity things. And what were they going to do with Vern and her after the bank? Maybe Vern was right—they really would be meeting Malcolm today.

She could slowly work her hand out the window and signal whatever it is you signal for help. Lower it and scratch "SOS" in the grime on the outside of her door. Maybe face out the window when they stopped, and mime "Help!" over and over with contorted lips, hoping someone happened to be standing there on the corner to notice, someone big and bold and yet caring enough to take seriously an old woman mouthing like a fish in a bowl. Or how about just fling open the door next time they stopped, and run, ducking gunfire. Run, leaving Vern to his fate the way he had long since left her.

At the faint dinging sound of the Preble Street intersection, she whispered to Vern to go right. And then, louder, over her shoulder, "You don't have to worry about us, you know."

"Who's worryin'?" It was Ray. "I'm not worryin'."

"Because, like I said, I don't see, to give a description or anything; and my husband here, he doesn't remember, so."

There was to be no reply. Arlie could tell from the zipping, change hitting the floor mat, he was still working on her purse.

"My husband must have thought you were our son," she began again, keen to keep some kind of contact, but not show she knew a name. "He thought he was stopping for our son."

25

"The camo? He been over there in...."

"I said, Shut up!" Ray interrupted. There was a sharp report, a whimpered "Ow!"

"No need of that, now," Arlie said. "No rough stuff in my car. No, he was...."

"You too, lady. Both of you, Shut! Up!"

But she didn't. "What are we passing?"

No, Arlie wasn't about to shut up, even to save her life. Without seeing, talking was the only connection she had. She didn't even know where they were any more. Her bare right arm was hot from the sun, so they were going south, all right, but she'd lost count of the streets.

"Looks like a post office," Ray said. "Big gray place, on the right. That a post office?" Then louder: "I said, Is that a fucking post office?"

"Shut up, you told me." The girl's voice was muffled— bent forward, she must be, face in her hands.

"Jesus! You're the one lives here. You want me to...."

"Post office sounds right," Arlie interrupted. "We're going good. Keep straight on, Vern, few more blocks." She could hear the girl sniffling behind her and went on. "No, not Afghanistan, our son. Way before that. Viet Nam. Before you two were born, I bet." They were still: not interested. Didn't even know what Viet Nam was, probably. But Arlie was determined now to keep them talking, even if it was about this. "Killed in Viet Nam, actually. 1972. That's when the war was good as over. His name's there on the wall, with all the others. You can go see it. Walk right up to it and touch it and spell him out with your finger."

Once more the car stopped, as if blocked by that long, tapering expanse of black marble Arlie could see clear as day.

"So how could I have been him?" Ray asked. "If he's dead. Answer me that, huh?"

"He don't remember stuff, Ray," the girl said. "Don't you remember?"

"'Membered somethin'."

"You don't get it do you, Ray?" And then she added, more resigned than vindicated, "He don't get it."

26

Arlie braced for another blow; it didn't come. She wiped the sting from her eyes. Ray must not be from around here, she thought: he didn't know the bank or even the main post office; didn't get how they were just tacking back and forth through mid town, going nowhere fast. The girl, though, she sounded local, though for some reason wasn't questioning anything. Soon, however, long before they'd ever run out of gas, she would have to get them to the bank. And then? To get them in close, Ray would make Vern parallel-park, something he hadn't been able to do for years. Flustered, Ray would pull her out of the car, steer her in through the big glass doors by the elbow, wait behind her by the velvet rope with his hidden gun pointed at her back and keep it aimed as she felt her way forward to ask the teller for all their savings. "In twenties, please," she could say, to make the count take longer, giving her time to grimace and dart her useless eyes and trace H-E-L-P on the counter in front of her in sweat. And all the while, back in the car, the girl would be holding Vern hostage. Not that that would be anything new for Vern.

"What do you look like?" Arlie asked. "Wondering if you look anything like...." Then, ruing the question: "Can you see Monument Square yet?"

"Coming up," the girl said, more brightly. "The bank out Congress we going to?"

"Yes," Arlie said. "That's the one. Out Congress."

She was running out of time now, as well as conversation, but the girl saved her: "Ray's like, really thin? Like your husband. 'Cause he don't eat right, chips and stuff, and he chain smokes, all the time. Crazy hair....."

"Shut up, Lee!"

But she didn't, anymore than Arlie had. "Your son look like that? Probably not the hair, though, in the real army, huh?"

There was honking behind them, and in the distance Arlie could hear guitar music, one of the buskers who played folk songs at the market.

"No," Arlie said over the noise. "Doesn't sound much like our Malcolm. He was a big boy. Big shoulders. From my side.

27

Maybe it was more the outfit. We have this last picture Vern loves. It's all framed on the bureau, him in camouflage, and every night Vern...."

"Make him drive, lady!" Ray shouted.

"He can't, Ray, that truck."

"Pull around it!"

"Vern, honey, can you see around the truck? Just drive around it if you can. Nice and slow. You see around?"

Stopping and starting, the car lurched ahead, then, with one defiant surge, the engine went silent. Vern was stomping on the pedal like a fire. More horns blared, overwhelming the music.

"God damn it!" Ray shouted. "Start it up!"

Softly, Arlie instructed: "Turn the key back, Vern. Then the other way. Do your foot." But though the engine turned over, it didn't catch.

"Fuckin' flooded it!" Ray snarled. "Get outta here!"

"Ray, not that way!" the girl shouted. "Cop!"

"Shit yes. Your side!"

"Police?" A pause and Arlie threw her arm back between the seats, grabbing cloth, flesh. "No! Stay here.... If they find Vern.... Vern! In the back!" She released his seatbelt, grabbed his shirt and wrestled him toward her. "Switch with him, Ray. Get up here!"

"You gonna....?"

"He's by the truck," Lee called, as Arlie felt Vern, whimpering and writhing, being dragged over the console and into the back seat. Ray's elbows, his buckle, gouged her left arm on their way forward.

"Officer," Ray said a moment later, his voice in the front bland and innocent as Vern's.

"Can't park here, you know. Loading zone."

"We're not parking, sir." Ray cleared his throat. "Stalled out on us is all."

The officer didn't say anything.

"So, OK I start it up?" Now Ray was almost shouting: the officer must have moved away.

But in another minute there was the voice of authority

again. "Need to see your license and registration, please."

"Is there a problem, officer?" Arlie asked, leaning toward the voice.

"I just need to see the papers, ma'am. Routine."

"This here's my nephew," she went on. "Grand nephew, that is. He's driving us to the doctor—in our car—for my husband in the back there. He's the patient. I hope this won't make him late." She opened the glove compartment and groped inside until she came to an envelope. She waved it to her left.

"License, too," the policeman said.

Arlie felt Ray shifting in his seat. "It's for medical research," she explained, smiling up toward the voice. "The appointment, I mean. My husband's part of a nationwide study and...."

"Back with you shortly."

"You all right, Vern?" Arlie called over her shoulder.

"Nephew?" Ray asked. But Arlie wasn't listening to him.

"He's fine," Lee said. "Aren't you fine, Vernie, all cozy back here with me."

"Just be a few minutes, Vern. Have to wait for the officer. You need the lavatory?"

There was a slap close by. "Hey, what the?" The raspy Ray again.

"Just wants a feel of your camo, Ray. Christ sake."

Arlie straightened herself. She took a deep breath: the heat there in the sun, the stench of exhaust, were making it hard to breathe. Or was this plight within a plight what made it hard to breathe? The chance and danger it brimmed with?

Hardly: it was none of that. Nothing as simple or logical or even heroic as that. What was making it hard for her to breathe was anger, the return yet again of the awful, inchoate anger at Vern for losing his mind; for abdicating everything, including Malcom, to her; for putting the two of them, over and over again, in jeopardy.

She grabbed at her wrist: "Two-Forty-Seven-P-M."

"Who's that?" Lee asked.

"So." It was the officer, back at the driver's side. "Seat

29

belt violation, and inspection's overdue. You've got two weeks. See if you can't start her up now."

Arlie reached across Ray's chest, leaning until her finger tips touched his door.

"Officer?" She waited, sensing against her arm the tension of young muscles, the held breath, the rapid taps of another's heart. "I just have to tell you..." and she waited again as long as she dared, "... that we thank you very much."

She sat back. Ray's buckle snapped. After two tries, the engine started. Air moved; the guitar twangs grew louder, then blurred back into the general hubbub of a downtown afternoon.

"Where you wantin' to go now, Ray?" Lee called. "You any idea at all where you want to go?"

Ray didn't answer. The car picked up speed, but two turns later began to slow, and with a creak of the emergency brake stopped abruptly. The driver's side door opened and closed, then the rear door on the other side. All was quiet except for the rumble of the engine and a slow pounding—the foundry on Grant.

"Vern? Honey? You there?"

Arlie reached back between the seats, groping until she came to a bony knee. She patted it, then turned and stuck her head out her window.

"You take care now!" she called into the dazzling darkness. "You two take care of yourselves."

THE RETURN

Except for the bruise, the fine inch of incision, it looks the same. As before. As the other. The smooth downward slope, the beveling up to the edge of the areola. The nipple valentine-pink in natural light.

She turns further, into full profile, straightens her back as in the days of good posture. The geometry of the thing. Of her. But she does not admire. She does not wonder. She does not, in all her nakedness, grieve. For the moment, she is removed. She is someone she may have met once.

Champagne glass, Clark had said. He must have read it somewhere. Or could he have thought up such an image himself? But it was true: her breast would have just fit a champagne glass. Still might.

The bruise is tender when she touches it. Of course it would be. But there is nothing there now. Nothing palpable, as the doctor put it. *Palpable*. She presses into the breast with the pads of her fingers, kneading the hurt, defining it, daring it. No, there is nothing there at all now. Save the hurt.

She looks from the mirror directly into window glare.

Bun is sitting on the unmade bed, one back leg thrust mightily upward. He licks his black coat, extending his tongue, his neck, to reach the long hairs' very ends.

She watches him. Watches him work his coat to a luster.

She lifts the breast upward. She cannot reach it with her tongue. She cups it, simple as water, in her palm. She lets it down slowly until it hangs free. *This thing is hanging on me, Bun. It* is *me.*

There, under the bed, is Figi. Only a tail, but it's Figi: the puffiness, the grayness. It flicks once, twice, and is gone. Smoke.

31

Sanders and Macaroni are curled in the far corner of the living room. Hardly any furniture left, but they still obviously consider it their living room. Rectangles of sunshine carpet the hardwood floor. At her entrance, the cats look up as one. Sanders mimes a mew. *Tell me about it, Sanders. You tell me all about it.*

By the front window she looks out over the rooftops staggered down toward the harbor. A tanker, riding high, stately, disappears past the jamb, heading toward open sea. Its tugs pipe jauntily.

What about the cats? Yes, that's number one, the cats. She needs to deal with the disposition of the cats now, while she's able. She doesn't know seventeen people, is the problem. Nor would they all be willing, necessarily, to take a cat if she did. Some might take more than one cat, of course. Or at least until other arrangements could be made. If they knew her situation. People can surprise you, how they come forward in situations. She would. She knows she would be one of the first to come forward. But she's not going into detail with just anybody. Not yet, at least. Pity is a luxury.

Come to think of it, though, she does know seventeen people. More than seventeen. Not well, all of them, but well enough. *And there are shelters. Like yours, Fullbright, remember? There they don't put you down. They find you good homes. They keep you until they find you good homes. Really they do.*

The sun is warm on her bare breasts. But the glass, when she presses against it, sheer cold.

No. Carol, Mom. Your daughter?

Carol! Oh, my God! I lost your number. You've got to come out! I'll pay your ticket.

Come out? What's happening now?

This place, Carol. I can't stay here another week. You've got to come get me.

What about Todd? He's right there.

Just come out, will you? This call's costing you.

Let me call my brother first, Mom, okay? Okay? Mom?

The dial tone nags in her ear. She hangs up. It is dark in the bedroom except for car lights swimming grotesquely across the walls and ceiling. Fullbright is a cloud of warmth in her lap, his purr becoming exquisite between her legs. Abruptly she spills him onto the floor and drags the sheet up over her shoulders with both hands. It covers her completely, like a shroud. Like the tents her mother used to make to amuse her as a child on rainy days. But, close as she draws it around her, it is no sanctuary.

Moya, it's Carol.

Carol, how are you? Where you been keeping yourself?

Oh, I'm good, I'm good. How about you? Still painting, I hope.

Oh yeah. Well, yes and no. Been helping Roger with the books more. But, hey! I'm glad you called. We've got to get together sometime.

Sure. I'd like that. But listen, Moya, reason I'm calling is I might be needing a favor. Cat sort of favor, actually.

Oh?

Yeah. I've just been to the doctor....

Uh oh.

Well, not too Uh oh. Allergies. He says I'm allergic to cats. Can you believe that? Me? Allergic to cats? After all this time? Anyway, thing is I may need to get rid of my cats and I was wondering, 'cause you always asked about them, if you'd consider taking one. Or two or.... They're no trouble, really. Fixed and everything.

Gosh, Carol. I don't know. If it was just me.... But Roger....

No, that's all right, Moya. Really. It might not turn out that....

Yeah, Carol, I'm real sorry. You know I'd do anything. But give me a call—or I'll call you—after the Fourth. Been way too long.

I'll do that, Moya. Putting it on my calendar. Call Moya. *There you go. And good luck with those cats!*

33

There isn't much on the shelves, but there is tuna fish. She makes tuna fish salad with the rest of an onion, and nibbles at it directly out of the aluminum bowl. Percy arrives first, rubbing his ear back and forth against the edge of the kitchen door, then against her bare ankle. In spite of his bad leg he springs up onto the table easily, landing without a sound. She feeds him individual particles of tuna. *Hey! Not so greedy!* She picks long, orange hairs out of the salad, puts Percy on her lap and strokes him firmly enough to contain him. He licks her fingers systematically, one by one, the rough tongue tickling their undersides. *You're an evil, greedy cat, Perce. You know that? Evil, evil, evil.*

She's got to call Todd. She knows he's told their mother she must stay in the home, as she has herself every chance she gets. But obviously he needs to tell her more often, and face-to-face. It's just that, the way Todd asks questions, they'd get to the biopsy, and she's not ready yet.

Percy squeezes back up onto the table, compressing her breast as he does so. She touches the sore spot as she watches him devour the tuna fish. Three women she's known have died, horribly, lingeringly, from breast cancer. Or the treatment: you never know which. Others are just out there with their dread, waiting. Dread lasts, outlasts.

She's not going to wait like the others. That much she does know. She'll keep her follow-up appointment, obviously. She'll listen to what Dr. O'Donnell has to say about the biopsy, ask the questions expected of her. But she's not going to spend what's left of her life waiting.

She stands and puts the empty bowl in the sink. Percy licks his lips, then the back of one paw. He begins working on his face and ear in serious circles of washing. *I'm not going to wait, Perce. You guys understand that? God damn it!*

Outside, she walks fast. Before she knows it, she's all the way down to Commercial, striding along the wharf side of the wide, dazzling street. Gulls are squealing like hinges overhead, engines rumble all around. Traffic is heavy: delivery trucks, dollies, vans, tour buses. Everyone is busy, even the tourists hurrying somewhere, as she is hurrying, somewhere. She knows none of these people and that is good: she doesn't want any reminders, any connections. From here on out, she has no past.

Excuse me. I have breast cancer.

She picks out passersby who have that look, that kindly look strangers can have. Of course, almost anyone would listen if she spoke up and drew them aside into a doorway. But what exactly would she say? What ultimately would she want of them? Without a past, where do you begin?

She is standing on the corner by the fish market, looking down the cobbled alley toward the harbor. Oil shimmers on the water. That would be one way, the harbor. After dark it would have to be. After the bars have closed, the cops gone back to Dunkin Donuts. She breathes in deeply the sea air, fresh as bleach. As her chest expands, she feels a tightness in her side, a jab of soreness. No one notices.

Of course I don't have breast cancer. I'm a normal person. How could a normal person have breast cancer? She is already down by the cargo dock, fingers laced through the chain link fence. A crane is hoisting crates, bright orange and big as 18-wheelers, onto the deck of a container ship. *My mother doesn't have breast cancer. I'm not on hormones. I've never been on hormones—the pill, but they said it was the weak one, and less than a year. No animal fat since Clark.*

On her way home, she stops at Rite Aid to buy two bottles of Tylenol Extra Strength Gelcaps.

She is not going back to work before her appointment. She has told them that at the office, but not about after, because she does not know herself about after. Working in the doctor's office is the last thing she would want to be doing right now. Plus, she would not be able to concentrate properly, and even though her job—filing—is sort of a no-brainer, you do need to have your wits about you.

She is quite sure about not working, but there is that whole thing about being around other people. So she's not a hundred percent with a plan. That's what makes telling the children hard. For that, she's got to be a hundred and ten percent. She will write a letter as a way to organize her thoughts, and then call. Not actually send letters to them—no one sends letters anymore and she's not an emailer—just call, scripted by what she's gotten down in black and white.

Cal is working on his paws again. Although Cal, or any of them for that matter, doesn't go outside, he always seems to be getting things between his toes. Probably because he's part Maine Coon, and got their extra toes. She can't stop watching the meticulous nibbling. When he's finished, she uses the plastic strainer to clear the litter boxes. There are three all together—kitchen and family room downstairs, living room upstairs—and they need cleaning almost daily to keep the ammonia out of the house. She knows that even regular cleaning isn't completely effective, no matter how compulsive you are about it, and that her paranoia about cat smell is one of the reasons she hasn't had people in for years. It's something she's not that aware of herself, even when she comes in from outside, but she knows the smell is there. From things Clark used to say, for one thing. She double bags in plastic, drops the lumpy bundle in the barrel outside the kitchen door.

As she is filling the kitchen water bowl at the sink, she becomes aware of distant pounding. When she realizes it's a knocking, she follows the sound through to the front and, after struggling a moment with the dead bolt, jerks the heavy door part way open. A man is standing on the stoop in brilliant sunlight. Clark.

What are you doing here?

I was in the neighborhood, as they say. Thought I'd stop by.

Just like that.

Just like that.

What do you want of me, Clark?

How about, come in?

She drags the complaining door, so long unused, a few more degrees, and steps back to let him enter. His hair has gone shockingly white, but it's still thick, and he's still slender. Deeper creases angle down from the sides of his slightly

36

bent nose. He's casually dressed, including scuffed running shoes, yet wears movie-star dark glasses with lenses the size of quarters. The dark glasses prove to be clip-ons, which he removes, finally letting her see the aquamarine of his eyes.

You moving?

Moving? No. Why would I be moving?

There's no furniture in here.

Oh, that. I sold some. Cats don't need much furniture.

He makes no comment about cats and furniture, which surprises her. As he wanders through the first floor, she follows him at the distance of a room. She feels like a realtor showing a house to a stranger. Only it's her house. Their house. After a few turns through the kitchen, a sort of inspection, it seems, he pulls out one of the two chairs and seats himself at the small table.

So, how's life treating you, Carol?

She stays on her feet, hands behind her, flat on the counter. *You must be selling something.*

Why do you say that?

You sound like people who call at dinnertime.

Well, it's not dinnertime. Is it? And, believe me, I've got nothing left to sell.

She watches him sitting there at her table, just like before, though he wouldn't have worn a tie-dyed T-shirt before. Wouldn't have spoken of Life. Fullbright pads in from the dining room and stops by the leg of Clark's chair. He gazes up for awhile, squinting like someone searching for a word, then begins to tease one of Clark's shoelaces.

You don't want to know what I'm up to these days? I think you might approve.

I'm not giving him any answers, she tells herself. No purchase on my life.

Well, I'm a teacher. I teach high school English. Always liked English. Guess you never knew that about me, did you?

Clark, I don't know what this is all about, but after ten years it's way too strange. And to be perfectly frank, this is not a good time for me. Not that any time would be. I'm kind of busy upstairs. When I come back down I expect you to be gone.

Clark leans over and flicks his lace back and forth for Fullbright who follows the movement intently, makes quick swipes, claws bared, at the curious, stringy prey. Carol walks past them smartly into the hall. She mounts the stairs.

It's dark. She can't tell which cats are on the bed. Some jump down and scamper off as she sits up. 9:37 on the clock radio. She is slightly hungry, or slightly nauseated. Before she can choose, she remembers. Cancer. Clark.

The first floor, thank God, is dark. The kitchen is empty; the chair he had sat in is pushed back under the table as if he had never been there. She toasts a slice of bread and spreads the last of the honey on it. She feels better eating it. She drops the heel into the toaster slot, depresses the lever until it catches.

She says out loud what she will write to the children: *Dear Blank, I am writing to tell you about some bad news, I'm afraid. I had a breast biopsy because of a question on my mammogram, and I have cancer. My reason for writing to you now, rather than calling....*

She is not sure what the reason is. It has to do with wanting to be exact and objective. Wanting to be faithful, yet not beholden, to so many feelings. Wanting to give adequate expression to an overview of life that she wants her children to know, but that she hasn't yet quite formulated. As she munches on the chewy heel, she wishes she had butter. When she is finished, she licks the crystals from the smoothly threaded rim of the honey jar.

Back in the bedroom, she turns on the radio. The stations are offensive, even the classical one. Especially the classical one. How obscene to play pretentious music like that when there's so much suffering in the world! There should be no entertainment of any kind allowed until there's no more suffering and everyone is free to enjoy it. She's glad now she sold her TV along with their furniture. That it wasn't all just about finances.

Clark is standing out in the hall. Because of the shadow

38

from the door, she can't tell which way he's facing. If he's coming or going. Or, for that matter, if it's really Clark. Would that be so awful, Clark standing in the hall? Anyone standing in the hall?

She makes little clicking sounds with her tongue. No one comes. They know she has no food, so why should they bother? They may be cute as kittens and grow into the look and moves of care, but cat brains don't have room for care. She's known that all along.

She sits at the card table looking at the note cards she's been trying to make. She can't imagine working on them now. She can't imagine how she ever worked on them, why Moya ever suggested she could sell them. She's no Moya. She has no talent. And who gives a shit about note cards anyway? She picks up the iris one. She tears it in half. In half again. Again. But there's a limit: it's too hard to tear through eight layers of rag paper. Her fingertips burn from the effort.

Sanders startles her, springing onto the tabletop. She picks him up and carries him over to the bed. Lying on her back with him stretched prone on her stomach and chest, she strokes him. He begins to purr. He can't meow, but his purr more than makes up for it, and the vibration resonates within her as if they were a single beast.

Maybe, of all them, Sanders cares a little.

Clark is lying on his side behind her, snugged in close as a chair. His upper hand is on her shoulder, moving over it in leisurely circles, then down across the upper breast to the one she's lying on. She feels the nipple tense under his deepening massage, then a pinch on the side of the breast. What is he doing to her breast?

She hunches up on her elbow. Clark is not there. Nor is the pain, until she lets herself back down against the wadded corner of the pillow.

It's light out. She has cancer. She goes into the bathroom and, sitting on the toilet, smells coffee. A neighbor must be making morning coffee, she thinks, though she's never noticed it before. She's not even sure who rents on that side of her now.

Clark is working at the counter in the kitchen. Although her bare feet make no sound on the linoleum, he must some-how sense her presence because he turns at her approach. *Still take your coffee with cream and one sugar?*

How did you get in? Wasn't it locked? She pulls her robe around her more tightly.

Oh, I never left. Except to go to the store. You didn't have a damn thing to eat here, except cat food. You haven't turned into one of those people who eat cat food, have you?

I told you to leave, Clark. Last night. Didn't I?

Well, you weren't very welcoming, that's for sure. But I didn't really think you'd mind. I got eggs and bacon and some kind of special grain bread. And the OJ with the pulp you like. Have a seat.

Carol sits down in the chair he holds for her, though she doesn't like being offered a seat in her own house. She counts six cats around the kitchen, variously sitting, lying, grooming. Captain is following Clark's every move with his good eye. They never hung around Clark before, but then he never did food things before.

I'm going to pick up some sundries after breakfast. He sets a champagne glass of orange juice on the oilcloth in front of her. *Anything I can get you?*

What's with the glass?

They were still up on the top shelf. Sort of special, I thought.

She sips the juice. Its succulent pulp is delicious. The rim of the glass is so fine it is almost sharp against her lip.

And, sundries you say?

You know, toothbrush, deodorant, razor. Don't you call those sundries? I'm getting pretty whiskery. Look at me.

She can see, now that she allows herself to look, that he does have a slight growth of beard. Reddish, the color all his hair used to be. He would look very odd with white hair and red beard and those eyes. A man who didn't go together.

Don't you have a home, Clark? What about Lynn?

He breaks the eggs expertly, dropping each with a hiss in-

40

to the hot, buttered skillet. *You were right about Lynn, Carol. And I dated some for a while, but that whole scene.... Maybe you know. You going to want strawberry, or how about this, what, ginger preserve I got?*

Strawberry's fine.

So, do you know?

Know what?

The dating scene—The Dating Scene.

No, she's not going to answer. Not going to let him know the extent of the damage.

He turns the bacon with a fork, lining up the strips evenly in the pan. *Yeah, I'm more or less on my own now. Which is fine. And they raised the rent on me, so....* The words morph into a shrug.

What about all the money, Clark? All your famous money?

He brings the plates with their breakfasts over to the table, picks Bun up off the other kitchen chair, puts him gently on the floor, and sits. *All my famous money. Well, somebody's pockets, I guess.*

And the buildings?

This one's all that's left. Not that it's actually left, *seeing as it's yours. You ever get it paid off, by the way?*

They prepare their toast, cut into their eggs, the yolks blooming golden on their plates. She pushes the bacon aside. Even if he asks, she's not explaining. About the bacon, the house, the furniture. Anything. She's better a mystery.

Way I figure, it's summer vacation, so what the hell? But how about you, Carol? Not a good time, *I think you said. That caught my attention. Or was it just a brush off?*

You know how I feel, Clark. Which makes this all, like I think I said, extremely odd. Extremely.

Well, I know how you must have felt. *But I have no idea how you* feel. *That's really what I came to find out. How you feel, after all this time.* He's staring directly at her, his eyebrows arcing over the upper rims of his glasses.

She resumes eating. She's not hungry in the least, but eating beats talking. It serves a purpose. As if in agreement,

Clark mops up the last of his yolk with a piece of toast and puts it in his mouth. More cats arrive, including the reclusive Figi. Carol doesn't know when she's ever seen Figi in the kitchen before.

I'm going up stairs now. Thanks for breakfast. Sort of.

Slowly she blacks out the petals with her felt tip, then opens the note card. *Dear Lisa, I'm afraid I have bad news. I've just learned that I have breast cancer.*

She tears the card into ragged strips, the strips into ragged squares. What made her think she could write all she has to say on a note card? Calling's much better, only she should wait until after the appointment. She'll know more. Like her uncle, Lisa will keep pressing for specifics, and she knows nothing now. She really knows nothing about her body. She can't even remember the names the doctor used pointing at the X-rays. That will be important, because he said there are these different types, but she's never been good with names. Her mother always said it wasn't a failure of memory so much as attention. That was one of her problems: she was inattentive, even as a child.

The house shudders: vacuum cleaner. She's never heard the roar of the vacuum cleaner from elsewhere in her house. Clark is vacuuming downstairs. Clark is out of his mind. Maybe he's on drugs, though he's not actually scary. Just, not entirely Clark.

Cats are slinking into the bedroom. They've never liked the vacuum cleaner, and now, with this new perspective, she can understand why. Cal and Macaroni jump up onto the bed; peg leg Percy jumps up onto the table. He circles in place a few times, then settles squarely on the little heap of torn-up cards and begins to lick the back of his bad paw. She strokes between the little panels of his shoulder blades. So soft. As if he's hardly in there at all.

The vacuum must be on the stairs, it has become so loud. The stairs act as a sounding board. He mustn't come up stairs, did she tell him that? Wouldn't a person know upstairs is off-limits? She closes the bedroom door without looking out.

42

She picks up the phone from the bedside table and pushes Speed Dial for Newell. The letter thing won't work for Newell— he's right brain like her. *It's me, but I'm out on my board, I hope, so...you know the drill.*

It's Mom, Newell, you there? Newell? Call me will you? Nothing urgent but call me? Love you.

She pushes her mother's button. After one ring, she hangs up. It's not fair to tell people over the phone, especially your addled mother, that you're going to die. Thank God Newell wasn't there, though children do expect their parents to die, even if they don't know that they do. She takes the telephone book out from the drawer of the bedside table and leafs through the yellow pages to Delta Airlines.

There are many choices in the recorded menu. In spite of the closed door, the din of the vacuum makes it hard to concentrate and she loses her place in the numbers part way through. Maybe she really is inattentive. She hits Redial and works through the branching sequence all over again, arriving, finally, at hold music. Something New Age. Should airlines be New Age? As she listens, she watches Cal lick between his toes. Periodically a voice breaks into the music to say that her call is very important. She hangs up, frustration feeling like relief.

The vacuuming has stopped. The house is still. She has no reason to go downstairs, but resents the loss of that option. Outside her door the coast is clear. She walks across the hall into the living room. Big Guy is draped along the front windowsill. He's the only one in the house—other than Clark, perhaps—unfazed by vacuuming. She looks out the window. Two gulls are perched on the chimney with the cock-eyed aerial directly across the street.

Why must some people assume the worst? She wasn't always that way, was she? That was an optimist who came east at twenty and married a Boston bartender. An optimist who moved to Maine pregnant, bought into the real estate venture thing. Had to have been.

I do not have cancer. I do not have cancer. I do not have cancer.

The gulls look all about, briskly cocking their sleek white heads against the immaculate blue. One looks down at her as if it heard.

Clark is gone. Everything is tidy on the first floor, including the family room where he must have been sleeping on the couch. That's a relief, though incomplete. In her situation, there is no such thing as complete relief.

He's not outside either, uphill or down. She walks in the direction of the office where she works, though she's not sure whether she's actually going to work or not, or whether it's even time to go to work. They can get along fine without her: a part timer, just enough for benefits.

It feels good to walk. She speeds up, walking up hill, until she remembers she has forgotten about cancer. She stops. How can you forget such a thing? And how is it possible that the sky and the gulls and the traffic and the people passing on the sidewalk can all be so fucking ordinary when just beneath the film of her blouse, just beneath the film of her skin, something so horrific is going on? Cells loosed by the scalpel are bobbing along in the currents of her blood to distant parts of her body. Liver. Bone. Who knows, maybe brain. That's it—why she can't seem to get a handle on things. She looks down, desperate for some outward sign of all that is going on inside her, some confirmation of her new reality, but all she can make out through her tears is the blurry outline of a slight, familiar self.

Up Congress she hurries, past the shops, the restaurants, the people moving with such purpose. She hates these people on the move, and yet suddenly she adores them: they're all there for her, every one of them, set into motion on her behalf.

She walks past work. The parking lot is full, as usual. She can imagine the waiting room crowded with patients reading magazines, at least holding them. She can imagine the close, windowless chart room where she works filing away all those reports, reading them sometimes, though she's been told, and knows, she shouldn't. Across town, in her surgeon's office, some stranger is filing her report. But a word catches their eye and they're pausing to read more, all the while knowing they

44

shouldn't. It's the one thing that makes their work interesting. The one saving grace.

She sits down on a bench at the edge of the park just down from the office. It is better to be looking at the office from a safe distance than to be in the office. No way she could do her work properly if she went in. Every word she glimpsed or overheard would make frightful connections. And not just medical words, but every single word in the language of this new land. They would puzzle her as the foreign always does. Alarm her. Certainly distract her. She would misfile things. People would die as a result of her wanton carelessness.

She stands, eyes fixed on the distant office.

I *don't want to die*.

Clark is gone. Everything is tidy on the first floor, including the family room where he must have been sleeping on the couch. But when she reaches the doorway at the top of the stairs she can see him in the living room. Or it must be him, lying curled on his left side among the cats in the sunlit center of the floor. Not only Sanders and Macaroni are there, but lots of them, maybe all seventeen of them. With him curled like that. Fetal. Feline.

She tiptoes into her bedroom. He has no right to make her tiptoe in her own house, even if it was his house once, even if he did work as hard as she, scrubbing and scraping and sanding and painting back in the beginning. She is not going to tiptoe any more.

Clark! She's at the living room doorway again. A dozen ears prick up at her voice, but he makes no response. She goes over to him and repeats his name, loud enough this time that it echoes throughout the house.

He rolls onto his back and stretches, smiles up at her, upside down. *Hungry?*

Pissed.

He gets to his feet, walks over to the windowsill and picks up the small woven-reed tray they bought once in Acapulco, and which she hasn't noticed perched there. *I made us veggie roll ups. And V8. Good for what ails you*.

45

You have no idea what ails me. Not saying anything does.

No, I guess I don't. He sits down cross-legged in the middle of the floor, working his bare feet under his knees, and sets out the plates and glasses.

She kneels facing him. She's not going to tell him. Then she'd have nothing left.

He peels the wax paper back from the end of his rollup, and takes a bite. *I would like to, though. It would make my visit here worthwhile. More worthwhile I mean.* As he speaks, holding the rollup in both hands, flakes of shredded lettuce sprinkle onto his jeans. With one hand he picks them up individually and sets them in a neat row along the rim of his plate.

I thought you had left finally.

No. I've been in and out. You were almost out of cat litter, too, did you know that? And toilet paper. When you're that out.... He takes another bite and chews. Carol peels back her wax paper and begins to eat. The raw vegetables crunch loudly in her head. The dressing is spicy, but good.

So, what are your plans, Clark? You must be looking for a place.

Not really. I've got all summer.

You're not staying here all summer. You do know that, don't you?

I didn't say I was. He takes a long drink from his glass of V8, wipes his lips with the back of his hand. He licks his hand before he goes on. *What I've been thinking is, I could maybe help you.*

And how would that be? Vacuuming? Shopping? Or, Oh, I know, you think I must be horny. Because you are. Can't find anybody else so why not give old Carol a try? An old times' sake thing, is that what this is?

No. This is thinking you might want someone to go to the doctor with you. I would. Want someone, I mean.

She sets her rollup down on her plate and stares at him.

It was on your calendar, Carol, in full view. Three appointments. Circled even. As if you wanted....

You son of a bitch! Get out of my house!

She slams the bedroom door behind her.

He is touching her breast and licking her ear. Only, the pressure hurts her breast, and his tongue is so rough. It abrades more than arouses. Loving was never like this before. Never had this kind of an edge to it before.

Lorenzo yowls as she lurches up on the bed.

Everything all right? Clark sounds so close that he must still be on the second floor. She doesn't dare answer.

She has the phone book out on the bed. Or she could just dial 911. She has every right to call the police on an ex closing in like this.

Minutes pass; nothing happens. She will call Todd instead. It's midnight, but he's a night person at the edge of the time zone. She should have called him long before now. She will tell him she is coming out, spur of the moment. And then, once she's out there, she will tell him everything. They've never been that close, being eight years apart, even through their father's slow death and mother's scenes, but Todd is still her brother, her era. They have a certain history. He will have ins with Cleveland specialists, though he may want to do everything, the way he did with the feeding tube. And Carol isn't sure she wants to do everything. She isn't sure she wants to do anything. Maybe macrobiotics. Two hundred Tylenol. But not a feeding tube. Todd has got to understand that.

She paces in her room. She is as much a prisoner in her house as the cats, except they don't know it. You're not really a prisoner if you don't know it. But what's worse, she is a prisoner in her head. Her thoughts are bars she cannot get through: straight and hard and just close enough together. If only she could squeeze between them she could finally turn around and look back in on herself from a distance. Then she'd know what to do.

There is a knock at the door. *How about a little warm milk to help you sleep?*

Go away, Clark. Go away.

The door swings in slowly, silently, and Clark enters, carrying a glass in each hand. *I know it sounds corny, but they say this stuff really works.*

47

He holds out a glass of the white liquid. She takes it. It is smooth and warm in her hand. Breast-like. She sets it down on her bedside table and shifts over toward the wall, giving Clark room to sit on the edge of the bed. He tests his milk with the tip of his tongue. *Watch out. Still a little on the hot side.* He sets his glass down on the mat on the floor. *So what do you think about Newell's plans?*

Which plans would that be?

Coming back to Sugarloaf plans.

First I heard of it. 'Course his machine isn't all that talkative.

Probably wanted me to buy his plane ticket, is why he called.

He *called* you?

Clark doesn't answer. Maybe he didn't hear. Maybe—is it possible?—he doesn't want to hurt her by appearing to be the favorite of their son. She reaches for her glass and sips the milk, which tastes sweetened. *I'm going out west myself, soon.*

After your appointment.

I'm not keeping the appointment. It's not mine. It's somebody you don't know's.

Oh, I think you should, Carol—keep it. We're getting to that age.

She lies back on the bed. Clark slips off his sneakers and lies back next to her, slowly, narrowly. It's only a single bed, yet he barely touches her side.

What do you think you're doing?

I'm harmless. He reaches up and turns off the bedside light. *Believe me, I've become quite harmless in my old age.*

In the darkness she can hear cat claws on hardwood floors. One of the cats jumps onto the bed, searches around among their limbs, then circles into the crevice between them. She can't tell who it is—maybe Big Guy from the size—but feels rhythmic pressure against the outside of her thigh as he licks himself. A motorcycle, loud as the vacuum, rumbles up the hill at top speed. Then all is quiet except for the familiar drone of Clark's snoring beside her.

48

She is alone in the house, except for the cats. She has checked every room and knows she is alone. She makes a bowl of cereal with yogurt and strawberries. Clark has left two boxes of strawberries from the farmers' market in the refrigerator. Farewells.

She will fly out to Ohio the day after the appointment. She will know what she needs to know, and can talk it all out with Todd. And then she'll be there to deal with her mother and can continue on out west to talk with Newell and Lisa face-to-face. One-on-one. That's the way you make decisions. And this whole Clark craziness will be ancient history by the time she comes back. If she comes back. Her only obligation now, as always, is to the cats.

As she's pouring more milk into her empty bowl, and setting it down on the floor, the kitchen door rattles.

Sleep well? Clark has a small white bakery box under his arm. He sets it on the table in front of her, breaks the string, and folds back the top to show her the contents.

Cinnamon doughnuts!

Cinnamon doughnuts. I'll make the coffee. As he gets out the coffee press and puts on the water, he tells her about the weather, which is cooler, he's glad to report; about his walk around the neighborhood. He seems quite animated and goes on about how he should have bought even more Munjoy Hill property back when they first got to Portland, and just held onto it. Ignored his greed—yes, she was right about that, too—and just held onto it. They'd be sitting pretty now, if only he had.

You'd *be sitting pretty.*

We *would Carol, you must know that by now.*

She bites into her doughnut, which is crunchy on the outside, just the way she always liked it. She hasn't had a cinnamon doughnut in years. It's funny, but you don't just go out and buy a cinnamon doughnut for yourself. It's not the same. She licks the sweet granules carefully from her lips. *You need to be looking for a place to stay, if you really don't have one. But you'll have to get your own newspaper. For the classifieds. I stopped it a while back.*

49

Oh? He looks truly surprised, presumably about his having to look for a place to stay, not her giving up the paper. He seems unaware of the water boiling over on the stove.

Whatever it is you have in mind, Clark, won't work. You wouldn't want me now anyway.

He doesn't respond, which is a relief because she knew it could be trouble the moment she said it: the opening she had given him. Instead, he rises to pour the boiling water into the coffee press. He stirs, inserts the strainer, applies the cozy. *I'll house-sit and look after the cats for you. How's that sound?*

They can survive.

Yes. Yes. He sits back down at the table with the press and two cups. *All those how many lives among them?*

They sit in silence, watching Percy and Cal lick the last drops of milk from Carol's bowl on the floor. Captain jumps up onto the counter. Bun grooms. Fullbright tries to get something out from underneath the refrigerator with his paw. There is the sound of scratching from somewhere upstairs. When Clark finally pours the coffee, Carol picks up her cup and stands.

I'm going to take a shower. Sleeping in clothes makes you feel dirty.

The bruise is already turning green and yellow, the tenderness is less. No lump when she probes the spot though in her mind's eye she can see what's growing in there, sending out its tentacles, its runners. Metastasizing, they write in their reports. She turns slowly, looking up and down her naked torso, and it's then that she realizes the phone is ringing. She peers out the bathroom door, dashes across the hall into her bedroom.

Hello?

Carol Fitzmorris?

Yes?

Just a minute, please, for Dr. O'Donnell.

The bedroom door is ajar. She moves to the limit of the cord, out of the line of sight from the hall.

Carol?

50

Yes?

Dr. O'Donnell here. Great news, Carol. No cancer.

The phrase hangs in the air before her: visible noise.

Thing we call a papilloma. Benign papilloma. Thought I'd call rather than make you wait until....

She steps back toward the bedside table, the voice dwindling as she lowers the receiver. She inches toward the door, pauses, her hand on the knob, and is suddenly running across the hall and down the stairs two steps at a time, scattering cats as she shouts.

Clark! Clark! Honey!

At the bottom she pulls up short. The house is silent. She lets herself down on the first step. Drops of water slide down her face in cool trails, down her chest between her bare breasts.

The house is silent. As silent as it was all those years ago when they entered for the first time, and looked about, and dared to imagine their lives taking hold in this strange new place and slowly, surely, filling up its emptiness.

HOME FREE

Quickly it came squirting out in his hand. Tom held onto the side of the basin as his knees buckled slightly. A minute later he pulled up his jeans and washed up. He wiped off the rim of the toilet bowl carefully with Kleenex and flushed.

He tiptoed into the living room and stood beside the coffee table. He stretched his arms over his head, nearly reaching the ceiling light, touched the toes of his slippers, spread his legs to the side as far as he could, and leaned out over first one knee, then the other. After a few pushups he rolled over onto his back on the rug. He looked up at the ceiling, then reached over to the coffee table for his clipboard. He drew three boxes around the word VOICEOVER on the top sheet and fell asleep.

Hen was crying. Tom got up slowly from the floor and went in to the crib in the far corner of the bedroom. He peered over the crib side at the little boy tangled in the sheet.

"Hey, my man," he said, "what's happening? I bet I know what's happening. My man is soaking wet is what's happening, am I right?"

The boy stopped crying at the voice, and at the feel of Tom's index finger probing the wet Pamper. Tom picked him up and carried him at arm's length into the bathroom. He stood Hen on the wash stand, broke the tabs, worked the Pamper out from between the boy's legs, and dropped the soggy mass into a plastic Shop 'n' Save bag. Then he washed the boy with warm, soapy water, patted him dry, dusted him with powder, and put on a fresh Pamper. As he worked, Tom explained how it was time Hen, being nearly three, should be doing some serious thinking about the wetting. So they'd have more time for things other than changing diapers, Tom

53

said. Fun things.

A little after six, after Hen had eaten his grilled cheese, Tom was watching the local news and turning the pages of the big Richard Scarry truck and train book for Hen who was seated on his lap. Hen was not looking at the book. He was looking at the news too. The phone rang in the kitchen.

"Mommy!" Tom said as he sat Hen down beside him on the couch. "Pad Thai, what do you think?"

Hen smiled.

Tom went into the kitchen to answer the phone, talked briefly, and returned to the couch.

"Was I right or was I right?" he said, leaning over to feel Hen's Pamper. "Way to go my man. Pee-pee time." He picked up the boy and carried him slung over his shoulder into the bathroom. He detached the Pamper and set him on the toilet. Tom waited, looking away.

Nothing happened.

"Got to be pee-pee, Hen," Tom said. "There's always pee-pee. Got to try my man, got to push push push like this. Watch Daddy." And Tom bore down grimacing until his face bloated red.

Hen watched. He made a face back. But there was no urine.

"Okay my man," Tom said, "you tried and I'm giving you full credit for that but where that pee-pee's hiding you got me."

Tom carried the boy back into the living room where Wheel of Fortune glowed on the television screen. They sat on the couch watching, Hen on Tom's lap again, sucking his thumb. "B" lit up on the board. Tom pronounced it, in such a sudden burst that Hen's thumb was jerked from his mouth. "Like this: B. B. Buh. Boy. Big Boy. You say it. Please."

Hen said nothing.

At the jingle of keys Tom and Hen turned as one toward the front door.

"Mommy's home!" Ann called out musically as she entered. Tom greeted her with a kiss and took the take-out sack

54

into the kitchen while Ann carried Hen into the bedroom, talking and hugging him all the way. Tom hung up her white jacket, weighted with stethoscope and index cards, on a hanger, and returned to the couch. He hit Mute and scanned back and forth through the channels. As he did so he could hear Ann reading what sounded like one of the Pooh stories to Hen, then kissing him good night.

They ate at the coffee table by candlelight.

"Felt dry to me," Ann said.

"Still won't go when you ask him though. I think that's the key. When you called? Dry as a bone. Perfect time, but nothing. I don't know, maybe it's me." Tom chewed another mouthful of rice and went on, still chewing, "I'm not worried though, not really."

"He'd pick up on it," Ann said.

"Hmm. They do, they say. Pick up on stuff. So tell me, who'd you cure?"

"Put in a subclavian. On my own. Smitty wasn't even in the Unit. And got this AIDS case? Won't take his damn cocktail. Sits there. Shade down. You know...*dying.*"

"How stupid is that?" Tom said. Ann slowly shook her head.

After they had cleaned up from supper Tom and Ann lay side-by-side on the couch and watched CNN for a while. They went in to check on Hen who was wet but didn't wake when Ann changed him. They got ready for bed and eased under the covers with hardly a sound.

"There's medicine," Ann whispered.

"For?" Tom whispered back.

"Wetting."

"Now you're worried?"

"Not worried I'm just saying."

"If he'd just stop wetting and start talking we'd be golden."

"We're pretty golden as it is," Ann said, brushing Tom's ear with her lips. "Don't you think?"

They made love quickly and quietly in the dark.

55

Tom was sitting on one of the benches, his clipboard on his lap. From time to time he looked up to watch Hen who was sitting cross-legged on the ground next to the low end of the kiddy slide. Hen was picking up colored bits of Styrofoam mulch that covered the central play area, placing them in piles more or less by color on the end of the slide. A little girl in a soiled jumper skipped over to watch him work, one sandal strap flapping. After a few minutes of study, she brushed all his piles off the end of the slide, went around to the ladder, climbed up, and slid down. Hen watched without saying a word. He made a face, to no one, then started back in with the bits.

A heavy-set young woman in tight slacks and tank top walked over from the bench where she had been sitting and jerked the little girl off the ground by one arm. "Ruthie!" she shouted. "Where's your manners? Don't ever let me see you...." She dropped the girl and detoured back close by Tom.

"Sorry 'bout that he yours?" she asked.

"Yeah. No problem."

"Kids," she said, shaking her head. "Who needs 'em?"

He watched the woman return to her bench and sit down. She stuffed the front of her tank top, which had ridden up over the bulge of her lower abdomen, into her slacks and picked up a magazine. At that distance, he couldn't see which magazine it was. The little girl was now halfway up the slide ladder again. She stopped there and leaned out to peer sideways over at the woman. The woman looked up and scowled, at which point the girl stuck out her tongue, clambered back down, and skipped over to the swings. The woman looked at Tom, contorting her mouth and raising her eyebrows, and shrugged. Tom looked at the words he'd written on the sheet of paper on his clipboard.

Ann was on first call at the hospital. Tom had grape nuts with banana while Hen ate fish sticks, dipping each one meticulously into a large bowl of ketchup. After supper they watched Wheel. Tom read Hen two books, including all the noises. He changed the diaper, wet again, before putting him down.

"You know, my man," Tom said as he did so, "it's okay to be wet over night because that's a really long time overnight, like ten hours. But when you're awake and you can feel what's going on down there and could, you know, do something about it, it's not really okay. Know what I'm saying? Anyway, I've been thinking. And what I've been thinking is starting tomorrow you and me we're going to have this schedule like every maybe two hours? On the potty. To be sure. No pressure. Everything's cool. Just to be sure. About the pee-pee. Deal?"

He lay the boy down on his back in the crib and pulled the blanket to his chin.

"See you tomorrow, buddy. Sweet dreams. I'll leave the hall light on okay?" And he leaned way over the railing to kiss the boy on the forehead.

Tom went into the kitchen to put dirty clothes into the laundry bag by the door. Then he went into the living room and sat down on the couch. He picked up his clipboard and read through the top pages, making notes in pencil as he went. He inserted a fresh sheet under the clip, squared it up, and wrote a few words before stopping and frowning up at the ceiling. A few minutes later he picked up the remote. He lay back and ran the muted channels.

Two women were sitting on one of the benches at the playground when Tom and Hen arrived. Three boys were struggling to get a rock nearly the size of a bowling ball up the incline of the big slide. They stopped from time to time to argue over the best way to do that. Tom took Hen down the kiddy slide on his lap a few times, then left him at his station at the bottom. Just as Tom was sitting down on his usual bench the heavyset woman entered the playground with Ruthie. The little girl ran directly to the big slide to watch the boys who were already half way up. Rather than sit down herself, the woman looked at Tom for a minute, looked back at Ruthie and shouted over to her, "I'm watching!" She walked to Tom's bench, glanced at Hen, then looked back at Tom.

"Cute," she said, thumbing in Hen's direction.

Tom looked up. He made a humming sound in his throat. The woman sat down next to him on the bench. "Mind?" she said. Then, leaning toward him, "I know I'm kinda big but...."

"Fine," Tom said, looking over at Hen who had stood up and was now walking toward the big slide. The boys had worked the rock clear to the top where Ruthie had joined them. "Hen!" he called, "Where you going?" At the sound of the voice, Hen sat down in the open space right where he was. He began picking up colored bits and stuffing them into the sides of his moccasins.

"Cute," the woman said again. "What're you doing?" she asked a moment later, pointing to Tom's clipboard. "You don't mind my asking."

"Nothing," Tom said.

"Looks like you're taking notes or something. On your kid. I'm not crowding you am I?"

"No, really."

"It's glandular's what they say. I'm thinking of going to the clinic for tests and stuff. What Ruthie's dad always said. But I don't know what do you do for glands if you got 'em anyway, huh? Ruthie!"

The boys had released the rock which careened down the slide and landed in an explosion of colors, and now they and Ruthie were sliding down after it en masse. When they hit the ground the little girl looked over at the woman. Hearing nothing further, she hopped up, brushed off, and walked to where Hen was sitting by himself.

"It's a screenplay," Tom said. "I'm writing a screenplay."

The woman turned back to him, wrinkling her nose as she did. "Like shows and stuff?" she said.

Tom made the humming sound again.

"You know what's really great?" she said, rubbing her hands together and squinting as she addressed him. "Prison movies. Like that guy what's his name with the bird and the little wagons like? Escapes and stuff 'cause you always want

58

'em to make it no matter what they did. That what your show's about? Something like that?"

"Something like that. A robbery in LA. Beverly Hills actually. Which you're not sure of 'til the end whether it's all part of a movie-within-a movie or not. Kinda complicated."

"Wow," the woman said. "You been out there?"

"Lived there all my life," Tom said. "Up 'til July, that is."

"Wow. You must be famous."

"Hey, I wish." He stood up. Ruthie was handing colored bits to Hen now, which he was putting in his mouth. Tom walked over to him and made him spit them out. He picked him up, and settled him into the stroller.

"See ya," the woman called from the bench as they began to leave.

"Yeah," Tom answered over his shoulder. "See ya around."

Ann was exhausted from her night on call. She read *Frog and Toad Are Friends* to Hen while Tom cooked a mushroom omelet. At the table, between bites, Ann highlighted a photo-copied article she had brought home with her.

"I've got a good feeling about our schedule," Tom said. "Of course nothing has happened so far but I really think he's getting the idea. What's expected. You think?"

Ann turned the page.

"About the schedule working, Ann, do you think it's too much, I don't know, regimentation?"

"Regimentation?" Ann said, looking up.

"Yeah. At his age, I mean."

"I'm sorry, I...."

"No, I shouldn't be disturbing you." He speared a mushroom with his fork. "When are kids supposed to talk anyway? That's more important really."

"Some kids are three or four. Churchill was four. Or somebody anyway, they told us in Peds."

Tom cleaned up the dishes as Ann got ready for bed.

"I'm really sorry, Tom," she whispered when he sat down

on the side of the bed next to her. "I didn't close my eyes once last night and that kid with cerebral edema? Dead no post. And I had to tell the mother. Good learning experience, Smitty said. You should've seen the woman though, Tom, I mean...."

Tom leaned over and kissed her on the temple. He stroked her long blond hair, sweeping stray filaments into silky arcs behind her ear. But she was already asleep. As he tiptoed from the room, he checked Hen curled next to the bars of his crib, then went into the kitchen and microwaved his mug of coffee left from the morning. He took it into the living room and sat down on the couch with his clipboard. He wrote a full page quickly, reread it, and crumpled it methodically, quietly, into a ball. He turned on the television, low, and watched.

Because it was drizzling, Tom dressed Hen in his rain pants, slicker, and rain hat and brought the umbrella with them to the playground. When they arrived, Ruthie was sitting on the top step of the big slide, looking straight up as she held on. The woman was sitting on a bench wearing a sweat shirt and shorts this time. They were the only ones at the playground and neither one had rain gear. Tom settled Hen under the big slide where it still looked to be dry, and went over to sit on the bench next to the woman.

"How 'bout this?" she said, as if talking to herself. "You'd have to have some kind of outside help but they shoot these smoke bombs. Over the wall into that, you know, place where they exercise? Only, one's got a gun in it and maybe disguises or saws or something and in the you know confusion and smoke, the guy gets the stuff." She finally turned to him. "What do you think?"

"Pretty good. Only I think those areas probably have screens over the top. For that very reason."

"Just an idea. Use it if you want."

Ruthie started crying. She was stuck on the damp metal of the slide partway down. At the sound overhead, Hen crawled out and peered up at her. He threw some of his colored bits at her. She picked off a few that had stuck near her and threw them back, giggling through her tears.

It started to rain in earnest. Tom put up his umbrella and handed it to the woman.

"Ruthie!" she called. "Get down off there. Can't ya see it's raining? We got to go." She stood, holding out the umbrella toward Tom and said, "You guys want to come? We're just over there."

Tom put Hen in the stroller and they followed Ruthie and the woman out of the playground. Less than two blocks away the woman led them through a chain link gate, up a cement walk to a low blue duplex. The woman left the umbrella dripping in the entryway and they all went into a large living room furnished only with a couch, a La-Z-Boy, a small refrigerator, and a wide screen television sitting on the bare floor. The television was on, muted.

"Not much going for it except dry, huh?" the woman said, holding out her arms. She turned on the sound and Hen and Ruthie sat down in unison in front of the set. The woman flopped onto the couch and Tom sat down next to her, on a blanket and sheet that were covering his end. They all watched the screen which showed a hospital room. A nurse was choking back tears as she adjusted an IV bottle.

Tom leaned back, sighing as he did so. The woman turned toward him at the sound, her full cheeks slowly dimpling with a smile. He reached over and began pulling up her damp sweatshirt. She started to help, awkwardly, then stood and led him through a doorway into a tiny bedroom. Nailed to the wall over a narrow bed was a Springsteen poster. She closed the door. They took off their own clothes. The woman handed Tom a condom from a low bedside chest, then lay down on her back on the bed. Tom climbed up on top of her. As he rolled the condom on, he stared down at the round contours of her face, her wide-open gray eyes. And, still staring, he began to root and work back and forth until with a muffled groan and whimpers he collapsed upon her.

"It's okay, hon," she said, patting him on the back of the head. "It's okay."

He slept deeply, but not long. As soon as he awoke he got up, pulled on his clothes, and went out into the living room.

"C'mon my man," he said to Hen, still in front of the television. "Got to go." Then he called out, "Hey, using the facilities okay?" He led Hen into the bathroom, pulled down the rain pants and Pampers, and set him still in his slicker and rain hat on the toilet. "C'mon, pee-pee. Schedule time." In a few seconds he heard the sound of water tinkling in the bowl. "Hen, way to go! We did it! Yay pee-pee!" He sealed the Pamper back on, and carried Hen out into the living room in the crook of his arm.

"See ya, mister famous man," the woman called from the bedroom.

Tom put Hen down and walked to the bedroom door. She was still lying there on her back on the narrow bed, large and naked and pale.

"I don't know," he said softly. "I don't know what to say."

Hen was already in bed. Ann made a stir-fry and served it with green tea. She lit an almond-colored spherical candle. The scent of bay leaves filled the living room.

"To mark the occasion," Ann said.

"I'll drink to that," Tom said, raising his cup.

"Now if he'd just talk we'd be home free."

"Right," Tom said. "I can't wait. Good title, too."

"Title?"

"Home free."

"For?"

"Oh, nothing. Idea I had."

Ann put down her chop sticks to give him her full attention.

"Idea for an idea more like," he said. "You know. Don't want to jinx it."

"Comme tu veux," Ann said.

They ate in silence for a few minutes, then Ann put her chop sticks down again. "You know this weekend?" she said. "I'm off starting Friday. After clinic. How about we take Hen

62

up the coast overnight? Some B & B like Camden maybe."

"Thomaston's got the Maine state prison, I read."

"Seriously, Tom. Be kinda fun wouldn't it? To poke around?"

"No it would, Ann, it really would."

"I'll ask around tomorrow and we can call—might need reservations. Smitty'll know places."

Tom sipped his tea. He looked at Ann over the top of his cup. "Wonder what he'll say."

"He knows everything, that guy. Amazing."

"No," Tom said. "Hen. What Hen will say. First. When he talks. His first words. Of his whole life."

Ann watched her husband as he explained his meaning. And into the silence that followed.

HOUSE CALL

"Dr. Wilson here, Mrs. O'Meara. What's the problem? At this hour."

"Come see Clyde."

"Clyde. He my patient?"

"Dr. Beaudoin's. When he still got out. But Clyde hasn't been out since...."

"Right, right. So what's Clyde's problem?"

"Bad, this time. Real bad."

"How so?"

"He won't get up."

"It's two in the morning."

"You coming or not? Edgecomb Road. One with the light."

"Not for not getting up at two in the morning, I'm not coming. I'm just covering, you know. Office opens at nine o'clock and ...."

"They said you made house calls."

"...at nine AM, Mrs. O'Meara. Or your doctor'll be back week from Monday."

"He's gotta sit here 'til week from Monday?"

"I thought you said he wouldn't get up."

"I did. He won't."

"Sitting *is* up."

"You think so? Not like this."

"Put him on, will you? And who is he to you again?"

There are scraping sounds. At a sharp report, Dr. Wilson jerks the phone from his cheek. His wife rolls away on the bed behind him, furling covers with her.

"Hello? Hello?" he whispers harshly, tasting plastic. "Hello? Clyde? This is the doctor. How come you won't get up? Hello!"

65

Silence, but for a faint tut in his ear—time elapsing somewhere.

Dr. Wilson folds his cell phone and sets it down among the change on his bedside table. He lowers his head back onto his pillow. It's cold in the bedroom, especially without covers: his wife is the one who keeps the window cracked all winter long. For their health, she says, though where's the scientific evidence for that? He gathers back what seems like his share of the sheet and electric blanket and tucks them up around his chin. Sleep will return soon, he has no fear. Unlike his wife, who always keeps an Ambien and a glass of Evian water on her bedside table—those time-zone defying calls from their daughter about her boss, or from their son about his custody mess—through thirty years of marriage and medical practice he has mastered, to her chagrin he has no doubt, the delicate art of dissociation, of distance. No matter the suffering witnessed, the prognoses told, the second guesses, the mistakes, the deaths foreseen and unforeseen; no matter the market sell offs, the reversals in their children's and grandchildren's lives or his wife's obsession with them; once his head touches that pillow and his lids close, he's on his way to the very outskirts of his mind. There's a certain door there he knows well. He knocks, watches as it creaks inward, pitches in the burdens of his day, and then, delightfully unencumbered, floats off into oblivion.

Only this time he doesn't seem to be floating off into oblivion. He listens to the warning bleeps of the snowplow as it backs and fills through the neighborhood, to the tick of wind-driven flakes on the storms, to his wife's puffy expirations beside him. Why in the world would someone call the doctor about such nonsense at two in the morning? Beaudoin's patients could be like that, though. They could use a little educating about how the system works. Covering doctors don't just sit up all night in their whites in some hardened medical bunker, one hand on the red phone, the other on the black bag, panting for action. No. They're whipped at night. Have families. Avocations. A life. The thing is, though, this O'Meara woman sounds like the type to keep calling back. The type

66

who wants her due. As soon as he's drifting off, well into delta sleep, the phone will ring. Put your money on it.

He feels among the change for the phone.

"Mrs. O'Meara, we must have been cut off. I just wanted to say what you're describing does *not*—N-O-T *not*—sound like an emergency to me, so please just call the office during regular office hours all right? You have a good night now."

"You're saying, what, call my son?"

"Your son? What for?"

"For Clyde won't get up."

"Call him if you want. But why? That's what I'm after. *Why* do you want him up? And who is he again?"

"He doesn't say."

"Who he is?"

"Why. Who. Anything."

"How about breathe, Mrs. O'Meara. Does this Clyde breathe?"

"Don't ask me; I'm not the doctor."

Edgecomb Road is close to five miles from the Wilsons', part of a World War II era subdivision on the other side of Veterans' Bridge, but Dr. Wilson makes good time: the main roads have been cleared by the plows, and at this hour the deserted intersections blink only yellow. Halfway down Edgecomb's double row of squat, frosted bungalows he can see, through the white veils swirling beyond his wipers, the single beacon of a porch light. He guns the engine, blasts through a bumper-high drift, and slides to a stop just shy of the garage. Bag in hand, he high-steps it up to the side door and knocks.

Almost immediately, as if from the force of the blows, the door creaks inward.

"Doctor?"

"Must be, huh?"

He bangs snow clods from his boots and enters a small, dim room reeking of cigarettes. Gradually he makes out stacks of cardboard boxes lining the walls and standing three deep on a table. A sink is crammed with unwashed dishes, while adjacent counter tops are landfills of take-out containers, ale bottles, crusts, jagged-mouthed soup cans. Cabinet doors hang ajar revealing empty shelves; and at his feet sprung mousetraps lie scattered on the linoleum among shards of glass he crunches as he walks.

As Mrs. O'Meara leads him down a narrow hall, a morgue of stuffed paper bags, and into the living room, he realizes for the first time what a tiny woman she is. Tinier, certainly, than the image her insistence suggested on the phone. Five feet tall at the most, he thinks, and, minus the plaid trousers, work boots, red and black flannel shirt, and pompommed ski hat, almost wispy.

Clyde—for that has to be he seated in the straight-backed chair at the card table in the middle of the living room—is the exact opposite. Leaning forward over the edge of the table to support much of his certainly three hundred plus pounds on his forearms, he suggests to Dr. Wilson a sumo wrestler poised for the clinch. He's wearing only a skintight Celtics T-shirt, trousers ripped up nearly to the knees to accommodate hugely swollen red legs, suspenders, flip-flops, and an oxygen cannula, which runs from his nose to a monumental green cylinder standing at his far side. A television remote protrudes from under his right hand, between a black rotary phone and a loaded ashtray; while a cigarette pack nestles in the pudgy curl of his left. Although the screen of the television against the wall in front of him is dark and velvet with dust, the man gives the appearance, by his forward lean, of watching it. On closer inspection, however, Dr. Wilson can see he's not watching anything at all: his thick lids are nearly closed.

"Clyde?" he says, bending down slightly and getting a whiff of stale skin. "Mr. O'Meara?" No answer. He sets his medical bag down on the floor, and tosses his gloves and overcoat over the arm of the nearby couch. As if in deference to the imminent evaluation, Mrs. O'Meara, who has hung back in the doorway up to this point, withdraws.

"Morning, Clyde!" Dr. Wilson shouts now at close range. "It's Dr. Wilson. I'm covering tonight. How are you?"

As he awaits a response, he swivels a frayed wing chair

over next to the table, and sits down. But before he can proceed, Mrs. O'Meara, knitting now in hand, reenters the room and seats herself in a rocker between the television set and a floor lamp. She reaches up through the fringe and switches on the light. It makes little difference in the general illumination.

Dr. Wilson asks, "How long's your husband—I'm assuming—been like this?"

"I looked in to hear the weather? Before that, musta been."

"And you didn't call until two."

"You say so. My clock don't work so good."

For the first time, Dr. Wilson registers the hollow tap he heard before over the phone. The responsible clock sits behind him on a wooden shipping crate, one of many containers he now notices stacked in the corners and here and there among the worn furniture. An antique clock it is, a girl on a swing painted on its face. Its slender, nearly equal hands point to just after seven thirty. Or could be six thirty five. Either way, hours—maybe years—off.

He reaches over to Mr. O'Meara's left wrist and feels for the radial pulse. He can't palpate one, but then the arm is a well-larded one, at an awkward angle. No luck with the carotids either, running too deep in the padding of that flexed neck. He takes his stethoscope out of his bag, sets the ear pieces, and steps the bell systematically back and forth, front and back, across the Celtics logos, listening for heart or breath sounds, while all the while watching for any tell-tale rise of the massive chest wall. As he moves in closer, touching the near shoulder gently with his free right hand as he does so, he suddenly feels the body begin to list away from him. He grabs around the far shoulder and with some effort drags the ponderous torso back toward the vertical. But when he makes to let go again, there's the same list, or inkling of it—a stirring more potential, perhaps, than actual. Ironically, it is this vague intimation of movement, of a quickening, which finally convinces Dr. Wilson that the patient he has traversed a blizzard in the middle of the night to attend is already long dead.

Mrs. O'Meara, rocking slightly in her chair, looks preoc-

69

cupied with her handwork. Dr. Wilson tries, as unobtrusively as he can, to reposition Clyde in such a way that he won't collapse entirely, taking table, tank and all down with him in one horrendous, and certainly unbecoming, debacle. But no matter how he tries to orient the upper body, where he aligns the short, beefy arms on the tabletop, what strategic nudge he gives to the accessible left thigh; he can not seem to achieve that uncanny, self-supporting configuration in which the man's parts must have been when he sighed his last breath; when the tension in all those exquisitely opposed flexors and extensors that hold us up day in and day out without our ever giving them a second thought, went, finally, slack.

To talk properly with this fresh widow, Dr. Wilson knows that he should give at least the appearance of full attention to her; should be prepared to move about the room in a natural, sympathetic way; should have his hands free to embellish his words with gestures where appropriate, and give that consoling touch at the crucial moment. Perhaps a professional hug, even, if it comes to that. But the saving rigor mortis might not set in for hours—the flesh hasn't cooled that much so far—and to ease, solo, such a massive carcass down onto the rug with any degree of decorum, any semblance of respect for the dignity of the dead and the sensibilities of the survivor, would be, he knows, quite beyond the resources of a fifty-eight year old sedentary, pre-diabetic physician who already hesitates to pick up a pre-school grandson.

"Mrs. O'Meara...?"

"He's bought the farm."

"Well, yes," he says, trying his best to conceal his surprise in a tone and look of empathy. "Your husband does seem to have... passed on." He watches carefully for the woman's response to his confirmation of the worst, but all she offers is a one-two yank at her yarn for more slack.

"I'm sorry, Mrs. O'Meara," he continues. "I'm truly very sorry."

"'T's all right. I don't hold it against you."

"No, I mean I'm sorry about your husband. I didn't know him or anything, of course, but...." Dr. Wilson shifts the position of his right arm to improve his purchase on the Alpine slope of the far shoulder. He can tell it isn't safe to release his grip, though his triceps is beginning to seize up, to burn. And his low back is feeling the strain, too, from the peculiar and sustained torque. He rotates his chair about ten degrees clockwise. That helps. If only Mrs. O'Meara had a little more heft to her, he thinks, he would just give in and ask her to lend a hand.

Instead, he says, "We should call the undertaker. Do you have a funeral home in mind?"

She looks up at him and probes under her ski hat with one of the needlepoints. "Bartlett's? Is that one?"

"Yes. Bartlett's Funeral Home. On Grand. I know them. Very good. Would you mind...I hate to ask you at a time like this...but mind calling them yourself? Now? They'll come right over. They're very good that way."

Mrs. O'Meara sets her knitting on the floor beside her chair and stands. "Kinda got your hands full there don't you."

He hears her scraping along the narrow hall. He hears her boots in the glass, drawers opening, her talking, presumably to herself. Taking advantage of his moment of privacy, Dr. Wilson lets go to stretch his arms, but as he does so he senses a sort of tectonic shift beside him, and has to move fast to recapture the body now slumping even farther away, its head newly cocked awry like a hanged man's. However, when Mrs. O'Meara returns holding a scrap of paper, she doesn't appear to notice anything different about their pose. She picks up the receiver and gouges out the numbers with a crooked finger. As she waits for an answer, Dr. Wilson prompts: "The doctor's just pronounced your husband. Could they please come out to number whatever Edgecomb Road. And right away. Dr. Wilson's waiting. So, *Please*, tell them, right away."

When Mrs. O'Meara has done as he says, she returns to her rocker. Dr. Wilson listens to the telegraphy of the needles and to the ticks of the clock marking time in its own world. He manages a glance at his watch. Three ten. A good twenty minutes, with these road conditions, until relief arrives.

"You want to call your son?" he asks.

71

"What son?"

"I thought you were going to call some son before. When Clyde wouldn't get up."

"Was I? You want a beer or anything? Don't touch it myself."

"No, that's all right." He knows he can't deal with another physical challenge right now, not even so much as the weight of a bottle, though the idea of refreshment, of any kind, has its appeal.

"Now, Mrs. O'Meara," he goes on, "if you don't mind, what about his medical history? I'll be the one filling out the death certificate. Where his regular doctor's away and all."

"Butts. That's his history. Butts and booze. B and B." She smiles, or is it a rictus?

"He have other medical problems—heart, sugar, pressure? On oxygen, obviously. Not so great with smoking, though I see it's turned off. You turn it off? After?"

"Me? He did sometimes. To light up. Not always."

"And those legs look pretty swollen."

"That's fluid. Had a lotta problems, all right. Had a lotta pills anyways."

"Could I see them?"

"If you can find 'em."

"You don't know where your husband kept his pills?"

"Lot I didn't know about him. Thank the Lord."

"How about in the bathroom, maybe. Where pills usually are. Or kitchen. Would you mind looking?"

Again Mrs. O'Meara disappears down the hall, allowing Dr. Wilson, with a determined heave, to right the body, and then some, so that it tips into him slightly, its new center of gravity transferring pressure from his throbbing arm onto his right lateral chest. When Mrs. O'Meara returns, she spills a brown paper sack of pill bottles onto the table.

"Son of a bitch!" she blurts as the last bottle rolls over the edge and onto the floor.

Dr. Wilson flinches, almost losing his hard-won mechanical advantage.

"What...?" he says. "How...?"

72

"You god damned son of a bitch!" Dr. Wilson's heart trips in his chest. But now he can see she's glaring, not at him, but, eye level, at the man in his arms. In a moment she turns and adds, in a voice so mellow, so eerily sweet, he thinks it cannot possibly be coming from the same person, "Forty two years I've been waiting to say that. Forty. Two. Years."

Dr. Wilson watches her sit back down. He watches the play of her fingers in the yarn, the only sign of life in the room. He is trying to reconcile things in his mind. Discrepant things like the agony and relief of death, son and no son, natural and unnatural illness, resentment and fidelity or something so very like fidelity that it would have to go down as such. He feels an obligation, if not urgency, to reconcile all of that, though, taken together, all of that represents as ponderous a challenge to his resources as does the weight of this body inexorably bearing in against him. Yes, he soon realizes, reconciliation is beyond him, at least for now.

With his free left hand he lines up the pill bottles strewn before him on the table: Lanoxin, Furosemide, Theodur, Zaroxolyn, Potassium, Trazadone, Micronase, Codeine, Prednisone, Beclovent inhaler, and a couple too smudged to read—all drugs quite familiar to him from his own practice, and indicative of serious chronic diseases, including emphysema and bronchitis, right heart failure, diabetes.... Curiously, though, all the bottles are empty, yet all those whose labels he can read have been refilled January 3, just the week before.

"Where are the pills themselves?" he asks.

"Must've tooken 'em."

"In a week?"

"Got me. His pills."

"If he took all this in a week, that'd be enough to kill him right there, you know. Even a man his size."

"Maybe it did. Or maybe he chucked 'em." She looks up, but with a look that doesn't inform Dr. Wilson any more than her words do.

Ten minutes have passed since the call to the funeral home. They must be en route, he thinks, but once here will they have the manpower to get such a generous corpse onto

73

the gurney and out into the hearse through the snow? Are the doorframes even wide enough? Is the cluttered hall? Should they have been forewarned? Well, he thinks, that's their business. He'll be well on his way by the time they're dealing with that.

"Chronic illness is hard," he hears himself say. "Very hard. On the caregiver as well as the patient."

There being no reply, he proceeds — he is, after all, curious now about the pills and the anger, as well as cognizant of the needs and often conflicted emotions of the bereaved at a time like this. Mostly, though, he just wants to get his mind off this grievous weight.

"And the burden of illness can build up over time. I see it often. Reach a point...."

"See that?" She is pointing to the floor next to her. In the no more than forty-watt light of the floor lamp, all Dr. Wilson can see is more broken glass, swept into a pile.

"Glass?" he says.

"Beer bottle. Tried to kill me. Tryin' to kill me all these years. And now look at him. Been killin' his own self all along." She snorts a little laugh, as if clearing her nose.

"He threw bottles at you."

"Bottles. Telephones. Lamps. Chairs. Not lately chairs so much."

"And why did he do that?"

"Keep me in line, I guess. Couldn't keep himself."

"You call the police?"

"You kidding?"

"You should. Should have, that is. Lawyer. Dr. Beaudoin. Somebody. Or leave."

She's quiet again. Dr. Wilson, no longer quite so concerned with appearances, struggles to true the body back up a little with his shoulder. The left arm flops into his lap, scattering the pack and loose cigarettes onto the rug as it does so. He leaves the arm there, disturbingly personal but serving, he's quick to appreciate, as something of a counterweight.

Has this woman poisoned her husband with an overdose of his own pills? Literally and figuratively given him a taste of

his own medicine? Or deprived him of them? She certainly
seems to have the motive—forty-two years is some history of
abuse. Could have timed the deed to coincide with his own
doctor being out of town, too. Or, still, death could have come
naturally—hypoxic arrhythmia, pulmonary embolus, coronary.
Happens all the time in these end-stage cases. You have to die
sometime, of something. A post mortem, including a toxicology screen, would show what happened, of course, revealing
lethal excesses, or equally lethal deficiencies, of medication.
Would show what happened, that is, if he didn't fill out the
death certificate himself, bypassing an autopsy and leaving the
ultimate diagnosis to the worms.

"Did he hit you? Ever?"

"When he caught me. Couple times is all."

"You hit him back?"

"You kidding?"

"Want to hit him back?"

"What, you sayin' I *killed* him?"

"That's not my job, Mrs. O'Meara. Just filling in the medical history's all."

"'Cause I wouldn't have waited all these years, now,
would I? To get free."

Now it's Dr. Wilson's turn not to answer. Not out of spite,
of course, because he is not the spiteful type, but out of simple
perplexity. He just sits there, canted on his chair in that mortal
embrace, feeling the musty flesh cooling against him, the ton-
nage sag and spread outward as entropy does its thing. He
knows well the catabolic goings-on of bodies at a time like
this, though he's never been quite so intimately involved with
the process before. If the mortician doesn't show up soon, he's
going to have to let him down. The weight, the mechanics, the
distaste of the whole situation, are getting to be a bit much.
And what does convention matter now anyway—decorum,
professional bearing? She hates the guy. Hates him enough to
have killed him. Would probably like nothing more than to see
him—all three hundred-plus pounds and sixty-plus years of
him—drop like a brained Angus. And yet he can't do that—
literally or figuratively let this man down. (What is it about

75

this night, this weather, this demise that has put him in mind of figures? Such figures are his wife's thing—double entendres, symbols, hidden meanings. Life as metaphor rather than as just, well, life as he has always known it to be, or made it to be.) No, starting from those first words on the phone, Mr. Clyde O'Meara, whatever his history, medical or otherwise, has been his patient. His charge. And when it comes to patients, *primum non nocere*. First do no harm. Even to the dead, he supposes, though he's never had to think much about that part of it before. Yes, Mr. O'Meara is his patient, to whom he owes not only proper respect but a proper diagnosis. Respect and a diagnosis to be borne into eternity, after all. He owes it to his patient to alert the medical examiner, press for the autopsy and the lab work, see justice done. Tiny women murder, too. Could he live with himself knowing he had abetted a murderess?

And yet, on the other hand, could he live with himself knowing he had let a woman be condemned a second time, a woman who has just this very night completed a forty-two year sentence? A woman whose life is knitting ski hats and winding a clock that keeps time only for itself?

She stands. "Must be them," she says, though between his reverie and his discomfort, Dr. Wilson has heard nothing. "Your keys in the car? To move it?"

He nods toward his coat, crumpled on the couch. Mrs. O'Meara quickly retrieves the key purse from one of the pockets and leaves the room.

There are scrapes from the hall. Crunch of glass. Rustling. The creak of the kitchen door and then a sense of winter air in the room.

Dr. Wilson hears the car engine start, hears it rev. There's the sound of reverse, then gradual fading of the sound altogether until at last he knows he is listening to nothing but the silence the clock makes.

ARMISTICE DAY

He was twelve then, living in a two-story house at the foot
of a long, steep hill in Cincinnati. Though I live far from there
now, he took us to that house once when we were visiting. Its
owners at the time allowed us—him and my wife and me—
into the front hall, but no farther. Standing there I marveled
that it was those walls and hardwood floor, that burnished ban-
ister, that high ceiling that had defined his youth. From the
look on his upturned face, I gathered he marveled too, in his
way.

There were also two sisters, and two parents, mother a
college graduate, which was unusual in that era, and father a
postal worker, sorting mail on the night train to Chicago and
thus avoiding war. And there were friends, too, of course,
chums like Dick and Clifford to "hang out with," kids call it
now, or "hack around with," we called it in my day; but this
was 1918, and he never mentioned their expression for passing
the time. Never thought they were doing it, more likely.

He kept a diary—quaint-seeming now, but perhaps com-
monplace for a twelve-year-old in pre-electronics America—
an old lined Record book I still love to read because, like the
frame of his childhood home, it housed some essence of his
growing up and hence, I've always imagined, of my own gen-
esis. Weather is there in those penciled pages, especially temperature and rainfall, and school with its classes in spelling
and geography, arithmetic and grammar, manual training.
Movies that he saw, too, like *The Legion of Death*, about a
women's battalion fighting Germans, and *Hearts of the World*,
in which French children confront world war; a special issue
of *St. Nicholas* magazine; books brought home from the library—*Careers of Danger and Death*, *Huckleberry Finn*, *The
Prince and the Pauper*, *Little Shepherd of Kingdom Come*,

77

Rebecca of Sunnybrook Farm. His jobs, the fading script reveals, included beating rugs, washing the bathroom, chopping wood, mowing grass, going up the hill to the store for groceries with a "sugar card" in his hand, filling out his father's time sheet; but "all work and no play makes Jack a dull boy" that generation always said (though I never heard him say it himself), and he recorded as well how he roller skated, played football, climbed on a railroad trestle, collected cigar boxes, kept nighttime vigils in his back yard for lightning bugs and shooting stars, dug trenches and built model tanks and "aeroplanes" with Dick and Clifford. Occasionally on a Saturday he packed a backpack and took the Anderson Ferry across the Ohio to Kentucky to explore and picnic in the woods.

One experience he noted in particular detail, as if in anticipation of a career still fifteen years off, was a week he was sick. Spanish flu he called it. Many people, of course, had viral influenza at that time—for six weeks school was closed, public gatherings were restricted, as they would no doubt be today if the bird flu threat materializes—and from his symptoms of fever, muscle aches, sore throat and cough, and poor appetite, I would have to agree with his diagnosis. A bed was made for him in the front room, he wrote, where he took sweat treatments and castor oil, Sedlitz Powder, a pink pill and a white pill, magnesia water and quinine capsules. For his throat pain he gargled and took sprays. When he had the energy he read his library books, but much of the time he only napped. The doctor came, nearly every day according to the entries, to probe and listen and conclude that his young patient was getting better.

The entry for November 11 is a long one. It tells, after dutiful recording of weather and symptoms, how church bells rang out, how guns were fired in the air, how flags waved as crowds of people passed up the hill outside his window heading for town. From that day on, as if it had been the virus in a front room in Cincinnati, Ohio, rather than the Germans in a railroad car in Compiègne, France, that had surrendered, he began to get better, just as the doctor said he would, and within a week was back in school, back on the trestle with Dick and Clifford and the rest of the gang.

In college, before I ever thought of emulating my father and going into medicine myself, and for no good reason I can remember now, I majored in French. To improve my speaking and sense of Gallic culture, I thought it would be beneficial to spend a summer there. My parents, cautious and patriotic citizens that they were, witness to many of the early twentieth century's dangers, including not only the First but the Second World War, in which my father served, the Depression, and the scourge of polio as well as influenza, had reservations about my plan. It was 1959; Algerian terrorists were on the loose in France. That meant little to me at the time, though in the world of 9/11, and as a parent and grandparent myself now, I can sympathize with how they must have felt.

In any event, my father did finally give me money for the trip, and for two months I walked and *fait l'autostop* from Paris down through the Loire Valley, across the Pyrenees to the Cote d'Azur and up to Lyon, stopping at villages along the way, sleeping on beaches, in fields or chapels, or at the occasional *pension*. The only time I stayed in a *pension* for more than an overnight was in Biarritz, and that was because I fell ill there and lost track of time. A flu-like illness it must have been, with fever, myalgias, and a profound malaise. I'm sure I hallucinated as well, my memories of that stay being mainly of foxes with huge ears running on the beach under Van Gogh-starry skies, and of children in long white tunics wandering in and out through my four walls as if they—the walls, or maybe the children—were no more substantial than the memories they would become.

In my backpack I carried a change of clothes, ground cloth, toiletries, the odd apple or heel of *pain-au-chocolat*, and, to remind me I was a student of French, a copy of the works of the surrealist poet Guillaume Apollinaire. Whenever I stopped in my travels for a rest, leaning back against a tree or the post of some farmer's fence, I would take out the book and read a page out loud. Though I understood little of what I read, probably not much more than did my audience of cows and crows, I loved the music of the words, the look of the text on

79

the page, the hints at the nature of the man responsible.

It was many years later, after I had retired from medical practice and long after my father's death, that I read something Hemingway wrote about Apollinaire, how, still a young man, he had taken ill with influenza in the fall of 1918, and died on, or maybe it was shortly before, Armistice Day. The longer one lives, I thought, recalling among other things how my father disparaged "writers," the more connections one is privileged to make. It might take eternity, though, to make them all.

ASHES

She knew it would be in the paper, just not what people would say. Even Betty and Kate, sitting at their usual table as she entered the coffee shop. Looked like her two friends had already gotten their coffee, their muffins. Of course they would have: ten past nine already.

"Good morning," she said, as she approached.

"Mary!" Betty exclaimed, an edge to her voice: she'd seen it all right.

"Oh, yes," Mary said. She sat and worked her knees into place between the table legs. "I'm not surprised, though. Not really. They all smoked you know, the worker men."

"How *awful* you must feel." Wrinkles etched Kate's forehead. "Your home. Memories."

"Well, like the kids always tell me: not mine to fret about anymore."

The wrinkles softened. "But still."

"And the new owners," Betty said. "From Atlanta didn't you say? Hope they have...."

"Coffee, Mrs. McCrae?" It was Jean, the retirement home's Friday waitress, wielding her two silver pitchers.

"Think I'll be regular today. Thank you."

When Jean left, Mary stirred in a packet of sugar substitute. Atlanta, yes, but that was enough about her former house: she'd just noticed Eleanor Winkler and her gentleman friend seated two tables away.

"Ashes to ashes," she sighed, raising her cup. "What they say, isn't it?"

Back in 1970, when Mary and Wendell had moved into their new house, people in the know were still calling the big rambling structure sitting by itself out on Surf Road a cottage. That Wendell even considered buying what he explained to

Mary was a classic, a John Calvin Stevens, had at first surprised her: the young nurse and mother still had no idea of all the options that come with a neurosurgeon. But as the furniture and orientals began to accumulate, the color schemes to evolve, the kitchen to lighten and modernize, the gardens and plantings to expand, she came to feel more and more comfortable with her role as homemaker rather than nurse. Just a new kind of caregiver, really. "There," she would murmur, children off at school, Wendell at the hospital, as she repositioned a chair by a window, "Better there, don't you think?" To a stunted rugosa, of an early spring morning, "Too windy for you, is it? How about over here in the corner?" And then to the rooms she still kept aired and dusted after the children finally moved out, and the echoes and perspectives of the big house had become almost entirely hers, "Just you and me now, it looks like. Just you and me."

That would have been the time when many women in Mary's situation, their homemaking and mothering done, their grandmothering yet to come, their husbands preoccupied with success, might have looked beyond the home for companionship, further education, volunteer opportunities, even a return to the workforce. But such a homebody had Mary become by now that such thoughts never had a chance.

Or rather, no more than once did they have a chance. That would have been the summer the Tall Ships came to Portland and Mary decided it would be a nice gesture to invite Eleanor Winkler, the doctor's widow, for coffee and to watch the stately procession down the ship channel just outside her bay windows. Mary had first noticed Eleanor several years previously at the supermarket, where her poise and smart coiffure set her apart from the other shoppers. Occasionally thereafter they spoke, and when they did Eleanor seemed pleasant enough, if a bit remote. By this time in her life, Mary knew that single people often feel out of place in a couples world, and she thought that by reaching out to Eleanor she might encourage her—and who knows, even herself—to engage in community life.

How surprised Mary was, then, when Eleanor declined

not only the Tall Ships invitation, but a follow-up offer to see her gardens.

"I called Eleanor Winkler today," she told Wendell late that night as he was eating his reheated supper. When he didn't respond, she continued, "The widow? Was hoping we could get together sometime. The two of us I mean."

Wendell swallowed carefully, then looked up. "What'd she say?"

"No."

"Good."

"Good? Why good?"

"Oh, I don't know. I knew Frank. Not sure she's your kind of person, really."

"What kind would that be?"

Wendell sighed, pushed his plate away. "You or her you talking about?"

"Well, both, I guess."

"Oh, I really don't know, Mary. Been a long day."

She let it go, as she usually did. Wendell had long days all right, long operations whose outcomes, she knew, were not always what he hoped for. But still she thought it odd that her husband knew what kind of person Eleanor Winkler was.

Before the house on Surf Road, home for the young couple had been a three-bedroom rental in Portland, where Mary began raising their four children and tended to her husband's needs and moods. Before that, back when she worked 11-to-7 at the Brigham in Boston and joined the roster of women Wendell courted in his second year of residency, home had been a single room in the nurses' hall. And before that, before the war, it had been a bungalow on a Lexington side street, where she shared the back bedroom with her grandmother, her stuffed animals, and her collection of 78's. A curious progression of domiciles it had been, culminating in her cottage by the sea, and ending—for now at age eighty what was left but ending?—in a one-bedroom, third floor, cable-ready, Seaview Retirement Community "unit."

If it hadn't been for the effects of time—on *her* as well as the house—she would have arranged to live out her days where she had spent the better half of her life, and where Wendell had taken his last breath. Indeed, as she had watched Parkinson's turn him to stone, as she slowly convinced him to move down to the living room couch, then to the hospital bed with its views of the fireplace and channel, more and more had she come to envy her patient's prospect of a homey demise.

But such wasn't to be her lot. The four children she had cared for all those years were not, apparently, interested in returning the favor. Of course mothering had never really been a favor, and of course none of them would have dared put it in such terms, but the upshot was the same. Times were different now, it was suggested. Distance, too, was an issue, as they called it, especially for first-born Charles based now in London, and third-born Murray trying yet another job, this time all the way across the country in Washington State. The girls— Aileen and Megan—geographically closer and traditionally, if unfairly, more identified with the care-giver role, had children of their own to worry about, husbands to please, in-laws to handle, careers to further, and none of them felt they could commit to anything more involved than long weekends or hired attendants. Until, that is, she should "decide to go somewhere." How unseemly it would be for their elderly mother, arthritic and widowed and unabashedly low tech, to live, and ultimately die, a recluse. And in such quarters: the roof, she must admit, would be no match for a real nor'easter, the ancient furnace knocked and stalled, noisy things lived in the walls, and she knew the plumber's cell by heart. And what about global warming, rising sea levels, if—and none of them meant it the way it sounded—she should live so long?

Megan it was, at thirty-seven the youngest but at just three states away the closest, who finally made the facility case to her, short-listed and chose Seaview, and then dealt with the Sotheby's realtor. At Mary's insistence, Megan agreed to hold off on the listing until her mother could make improvements she said would not only increase the value of the property but honor the responsibility she felt, if couldn't explain, toward it. And hadn't they all said it needed work?

Third day on the market, the place sold. It was May, the

cottage at its most classic, the daffodils a riot of yellow, the songbirds twittering their hearts out. Should have asked more, Mom, the older kids said when they heard the closing price. No, Mary reassured them, fine with me. They're a young family, from Atlanta, I hear. It'll be us all over again.

Even with the help of the children, of movers and appraisers and a slug of cortisone in both knees, it took Mary over a month to process her nearly eight decades' worth of possessions—divvy up what was to be divvied up, sell what was to be sold, donate what was to be donated, toss what was to be tossed—and shoe-horn into her new, diminutive lodgings what was left. The heirlooms, pictures, and mementos Megan and she selected installed, the last of the papers signed, the children and grandchildren seen off in their rental cars, she took to her new bed, pulled up her grandmother's throw, and awaited the Reaper.

And awaited. And awaited. Delores Randall, the widow of a lawyer who had apparently defended Wendell a time or two in the past, took her under her wing, introduced her to her own circle of Seaview friends and gave a tour of the grounds, the shuffle board court, the beauty shop, the library and auditorium. Three women from the old neighborhood had her in for tea, but she'd been so tied up with house and children and then, those last few years, Wendell, that she'd paid little attention to neighbors, and now they seemed, on re-acquaintance, stranger than real strangers. Betty Hauser, across the hall, invited her to morning coffee in the coffee shop, where she met Betty's friend Kate Ochoa, a woman seeming constantly on the verge of tears, though she blamed allergies. Kate and Betty, it turned out, had been meeting in the coffee shop for breakfast for two years; it wasn't long before Mary was joining them regularly. And then for dinner most nights as well.

And how grateful for that she became, once she realized that one of her white-haired, stooped peers, one of the two hundred and fifty souls fate had cast her lot with, was none other than Eleanor Winkler. Though Eleanor usually took her meals with a widower recently moved down from Machias, and it was thus natural for the other single women to keep their distance, there was always the off chance of an elevator encounter, a musical program seating, a casual introduction in the lobby. Should that happen, would she dare say anything?

Mid-July it was that Mary, convinced that the Reaper must have more pressing business, allowed herself thoughts of her former house. She still had the old Park Avenue, its trunk still loaded with Wendell's emergency equipment—jumper cables, flares, flashlight, foil blankets, matches, gas can. All those years of house calls and trips to the ski lodge, he'd never once had to use any of it, but even when Wendell's and her driving had been reduced to fair-weather runs to the super market, Wendell wouldn't get rid of it. Now that she could, she didn't dare: it was still somehow his. And as he always said, you never know.

Curiously, as she approached it, the old homestead looked much as it had when Megan had driven her off that last time. No curtains at the windows, disassembled trampoline by the garage, the trash barrel still overflowing with the wood scraps they'd cleaned out from Wendell's workshop. Driving by slowly, one eye on the rear view mirror, she could take in only so much, but enough to suggest that her departure had brought local time to a stop.

At coffee a few mornings later, Betty asked if she'd ever been back by the old house. Coincidence? Did Betty know things?

"Did drive by the other day, actually. Old times' sake. You know how that is."

"Indeed I do. Must have been strange, though."

Kate wiped an eye and leaned forward to venture, "Did you go in?"

"Go in?" Mary replied. "You can't go in anymore."

"She's right, Kate. But did you...?"

"Besides," Mary interrupted, but no besides came to mind.

For almost another week she managed to stay away. And when she returned she did see change—a huge, rusted dump-ster angled across the lawn and onto the driveway like some random hunk of space junk. When she reached the stretch of road beyond, where the shoulder widened onto a full view of the ocean, she pulled over sharply. Something knocked in the trunk.

Dumpster? What would you need a dumpster for? Hadn't she gotten rid of everything that wasn't nailed down, and much that was? Even had the cleaning company back for a last go-round? She needed to talk to somebody. But the kids would tell her to mind her own business. She didn't feel that safe with anyone at Seaview yet, not even—or maybe especially— Betty and Kate. And the new owners—well, the lawyer had made it very clear about her and the new owners.

Over the next few weeks Mary made regular trips down Surf Road, no longer slowing and no longer needing to: she could see plenty at the speed limit. The entire front lawn had become a parking lot for pickups and flatbeds. Workmen dotted the roofs and hung off the walls. The screech of saws, the thuds of hammers, the clap of falling boards filled the air. Hard-hats came and went through a widened front door, toting beams and barn boards and whole sheets of parquet flooring toward the dumpster. Windows became jagged maws, the cedar shingles went, new gables hatched and old ones shifted or morphed into skylights and domes, cement mixers backed over the rhododendrons to the south of the house, and to the north another foundation began connecting the garage to Wendell's once den. On bright days, she could see right through to the sun glittering on the channel and the islands beyond. As if the house were—had perhaps always been—a mere facade.

Finally, after Labor Day, she could stand it no longer. She bumped in over the ruts, parked behind a Classic Kitchens truck, and clambered up onto an extension of the front porch.

"Help you, lady?" a workman said, pulling a face mask down onto his beard.

"What's going on here?"

"What's going on? Who wants to know?" He fished a pack from his shirt pocket and tapped out a cigarette.

"I lived here."

"Good for you. Wanna have a look-see?"

"I've *had* a look-see. I want to know what's going on."

He stabbed his cigarette toward her. "What you want is talk to the foreman."

She turned and climbed down off the porch, "Around the side!" ringing in her ears. Backing out onto Surf she nearly hit a delivery van, dipped into the ditch across the road, and gunned it south.

That night the desk called: she hadn't shown up at dinner or cancelled, as per the rules. "No, don't send anything up," she said. "Eating in tonight."

But she wasn't eating in tonight. She was rocking back and forth on her bed as she walked the first floor, climbed the front stairs, entered her old rooms one after the other, caressing the jambs and the sills and the furnishings as she passed, mourning and treasuring all at once.

There's right, and there's right, she explained to her old haunts. She'd gone along with everything in life so far. Done her parents' bidding, her profession's, Wendell's, the children's, Wendell's again, the children's again. A lifetime of going along, really. And that was fine. Because, up to now, it had all been expected. Isn't that all right is?

Every few years Wendell, speaking as one who had taken care of his share of vehicle-related head injuries, had petitioned the town for better street lights on their road. It had been his one venture into civic life, but in spite of his efforts and the respect he enjoyed in the community, nothing had ever come of it. Now Mary was glad nothing had. And turning into the driveway, she could see there were no lights at the house itself. She pulled in along side the dumpster and turned off the engine. High above the great steel box the scatter-glow of the moon outlined the roof. A tiny light was moving eastward past the peak—the eleven o'clock to England, probably, where Charles, oblivious as ever and as the rest of them, would be waking soon.

"Look at you, poor thing," she murmured as she stepped out. The air off the water was cool and damp, the way it always was come early fall. She pulled her sweater around her as she made her way to the back of the car. She opened the trunk and rummaged through the jumbled supplies until she found Wendell's flashlight. Amazingly, it still worked, and by its beam she picked her way through the debris of nails and shingles, tarps and cigarette butts, up onto the porch. The massive new front door was locked, but further along the wall she came to one of the new windows. It was open. Backing herself up onto the sill, she hiked her dress, bent head to knees as far as pain allowed, and swiveled in.

But had she entered through a window or a looking glass? No matter where she aimed her beam, no matter where she stepped, nothing made sense. Skewed or missing were the walls she had personally papered and painted, gone were the beams from the ceiling. Gone too the kitchen of those countless meals—or was all that stainless steel someone's idea of a kitchen? A circular staircase filled her old entryway, and the floor, the parquetry of her years of care, had given way to a vast hardwood rink. The only thing she could recognize was the moonlight sparkling on the water out the eastern windows, like a fire in a grate.

She left the way she had come, following her light across the uneven ground all the way to the open trunk.

BEDSIDE MANNERS

Margaret was thrilled at the prospect of a house call. Well, maybe thrilled isn't exactly the right word if your husband has really reached that point, but compared to everything else that had been happening recently, the offer certainly came as a relief.

It had been weeks now that Charles had not been right. At first, neither of them had dared suggest it could be the cancer coming back, but when he'd lost another five pounds, and needed the windows open to breathe, she knew she had to say something. He finally agreed she could call the doctor, and, despite the effort involved, went in for the blood work and full-body scan. When Dr. Whiting phoned that evening with the results, all Charles said was that he hadn't gone into specifics. Would make a house call, though, to go over the details.

Margaret had seen Travis Whiting only once before, three years previously, when the original referral had been made. From then on, Charles had insisted on keeping his appointments for radiation and chemo and follow-up on his own, even when the heartburn and the nausea got to him. That had bothered Margaret at first, but she knew how much pride her husband took in his self-sufficiency, and who knows, she thought, pride might just give him that extra edge. In any event, something must have: within weeks his breathing had improved, his weight had picked up, the scans had cleared, and there he was, back to his old self. Just in case, though, neither mentioned the C word or the distant fifth anniversary when, they'd been told, they could start mentioning that other C word, cure. They returned to church, where, it seemed to Margaret, Charles rendered the hymns more earnestly than he ever had before. They resumed their trips to major-league stadiums and twice trav-

91

elled to the Viet Nam Veterans Memorial in Washington where Charles said a prayer—said something, anyway—before the names of two of his old buddies. Retired, reasonably well pensioned, child-free, winners, they were beginning to believe, of life's only important lottery, they could do pretty much anything they wanted. And then this.

Though Margaret thought she was prepared for Dr. Whiting's visit late that Tuesday afternoon, when he actually stepped through the front door she realized she wasn't at all. Tall and fit as she remembered, he now evinced a power she must have overlooked back in the medical center setting. Whether it was the perspective of her humble front hall, the contrast with Charles' frailty, and by extension her own, or the vast reserves of medical knowledge she now knew waited behind that high, smooth brow, she didn't know. Only that she was totally in thrall to the man.

He stayed a good hour, explaining, with occasional sketches on prescription blanks, the results of the blood work and scan; then reviewing staging terms, therapeutic options with their statistics, their pros and cons. Doing nothing was an option, too, he said, its own special kind of therapy. And no matter what they decided, if things progressed he was quite sure that, along with hospice and the entire oncology team, he would be able to keep Charles comfortable, and at home if they so desired. Why didn't they think things over for a few days—there was no emergency about any of this—talk with friends and family, involve their spiritual, legal, and financial advisors as appropriate. A second opinion, too, would be fine, easily arranged. He would order oxygen and a mild relaxant for now, and would return at the end of the week to see how their thoughts were progressing. He didn't want to overstay his welcome, but did they have any questions at this point?

Charles didn't, or any that he asked anyway. And Margaret had only one, which she managed to keep to herself—how could a doctor, how could any human being, be so utterly magnificent?

Unfortunately, Charles didn't respond much when Margaret brought up the doctor's visit over the next few days. She did manage to get the minister in one afternoon, but neither man confided much about their discussion afterwards, and she ended up doing most of her talking with her friend Ruth. As much as she hated to leave Charles for something as trivial sounding as coffee, she was that desperate to pursue the crucial issues facing them. She was also desperate to express her admiration for Dr. Whiting. And though Ruth had never been one to offer a lot of specific advice or comment, she listened well, and right now that was exactly what Margaret felt she needed.

When the doctor returned late Friday, he checked the oxygen settings, asked Charles about symptoms, listened to his chest, and mentioned a call he'd made to the cancer center in Boston about the case. So subtly did he then move on to the question of treatment that before Margaret even realized it Charles was announcing his decision—none. Stunned, she could only watch as Dr. Whiting made a place for himself on the side of the bed, got out his prescription pad, and started in on comfort-care plans.

Even after the doctor left, all Margaret could manage was, Why? What she was after, of course, was, Why didn't you discuss this with me? What Charles seemed to have heard, though, was, Why don't you want to be treated? It just felt right this time, he said. Natural. Dignified. Dignified? Margaret asked, unable to make it sound remotely like a question. What's dignity got to do with it? He didn't answer, which she didn't really expect him to. No doubt it all went back to Viet Nam, the horrors, the camaraderie he'd known there long before he knew her, and had treasured deep inside ever since. Something about not making a fuss over yourself, even under fire. Something about accepting the absurd. For her, though, she was beginning to suspect, it was something about festering into malignancy.

So be it. Given the doctor's odds, what chance did they have, really, for a second miracle? But if her husband wasn't going to have the solace of hope this time around, he'd still have to have the solace of something. Two nights later Margaret suggested they pray together. Charles seemed fine with

93

that, and though not offering words of his own, added a serviceable Amen when Margaret finished with hers. She even asked the minister to resume visits, though what good that did she wasn't sure either as he always saw Charles alone. At times like this, the minister explained to her, it's the one-on-ones with God that count.

All the while, the medical presence in the house was growing. Once a week an oncology nurse came to check the pain scale, vital signs, skin condition, oral hygiene, nutrition, and to reconfigure the bedroom yet again. A commode arrived, followed by an electric bed with trapeze and foam pads. Suppressants were started for the cough that was beginning to interrupt Charles' sleep. A liquid pain concoction was placed on his bedside table just in case. And every other week, as promised, Dr. Whiting visited as well. For his examination, he would ask Margaret to step out, though she didn't understand why that was necessary for a wife of over forty years. Or why the examination took so long, longer even, sometimes, than the minister's visits. One day after the doctor had left, she asked Charles about that. All he would say was that the man was thorough.

As the weeks passed, Margaret grew increasingly anxious, not about her husband's slow deterioration, which she expected and understood, or her own imminent widowhood, for which his habit of privacy was at least some preparation, but about the fact that the time for the two of them truly to connect was fast running out. Theirs had been a reasonably happy and, in the early years at least, passionate relationship, but had never progressed to that ecstatic fusion of souls she had always thought marriage implied. That was not something one experienced right off the bat, of course, but gradually achieved, after the child decisions and the army retirement decisions and the contractor business decisions and the aging parent decisions had all been sorted through. And then the first cancer treatments, coming as they did just months after Charles' retirement, hardly seemed the occasion for such a consummation: heart-to-hearts about existential matters and the afterlife might not only divert his attention, but actually jinx the outcome. And then, of course, when the good news came, all she could think of was celebration and getting her house back. This time around though, there was no prognosis to jinx, no future to defer to. Twice she did manage to ask what he was thinking about as he lay there in the bed, eyes half-closed, television dark, newspaper furled by his side. Not much, was all he offered. No pain or anything. How do you follow that up, she wondered? Which of her urgent questions and sentiments did she dare trouble him with?

One afternoon about six weeks later, as Margaret was seeing Dr. Whiting out after his visit, he turned to her and in a low voice said she might want to keep that bottle of pain medication out of sight. Why was that, she asked? The suicidal thoughts, he said. Oh, that, she replied. Of course.

Suicidal thoughts? Certainly some degree of depression would be appropriate for a dying man. It was a stage, she'd read somewhere, on the road from anger to acceptance. But suicide? Charles? Nothing she asked or suggested to him over the next few days brought out anything more than a hint of understandable fatalism. Even when she alluded to her own grief, he offered nothing about his own, and nothing in the way of consolation. But did he know he was depriving her of the one solace she might have had in this awful situation, of the ultimate intimacy she must deserve by now? The more she thought about it, the more deprived, in fact, she felt, and the more deprived she felt, the more angry she grew. When they prayed together now, she mentioned this to God in code, asking that He help them rise above any negative feelings that might be tempting them in their situation.

However, just as she hadn't wanted to admit to the doctor that Charles had never confided anything to her about suicidal thoughts—about any thoughts, for that matter—Margaret wasn't quite ready to let her husband know what the doctor had told her. She didn't want to squander that knowledge, nor did she want to be seen as using it on him. How was an old soldier going to reconcile suicidal thoughts with just fading away?

Ruth, it turned out, had had some experience with such

thoughts in a sister-in-law, and said the thing about depressives was that deep down they were ashamed of their feelings and wanted to hide them, except from one safe person. If that one safe person in Charles' case was the doctor, especially such a wonderful one as Margaret had made him out to be, then maybe she should just leave well enough alone. Margaret was so surprised, almost offended, that after all these years her friend had actually come up with advice, that she immediately dismissed it.

Still hopeful that Dr. Whiting was wrong about the depth of the depression, or rather that he hadn't bonded with her husband more deeply in weeks than she had in decades, she decided to test their doctor-patient relationship further. How much help, she asked him at the next visit, did he think Charles' faith was to him. Regarding the suicidal thoughts. Faith? the doctor replied, pausing to let the shadow of a wrinkle pass across his brow. Not really a term your husband uses much is it.

The next morning, after giving Charles his custard and tea, Margaret broke the news: Dr. Whiting had been called out of town indefinitely because of family illness. She sat with him quietly for a few more minutes, before asking how he felt about that. All right, he said. Not much he can really do now anyway. Margaret gave him a kiss, then went downstairs to the kitchen phone. Charles had died in the night, she told Dr. Whiting. Very peaceful. For the best, she knew. Dr. Whiting said he wasn't surprised, just at the timing, and agreed it was for the best. How wonderful that Charles had been able to take his last breath in his own home, in the presence of such a devoted wife.

Back in the bedroom, Margaret sat down on the edge of the bed, adjusted the oxygen tubing and, one hand stroking her husband's arm, began: Charles, honey, can we talk?

DELIVERY

One evening during my sophomore year in high school, as I was heading up to my room to do my homework, my father called to me. I cringed because, as my grades had been slipping recently, he had taken to spot-checking my assignments. Not only was it painful to have my mistakes pointed out, but, at age fifteen, embarrassing to have my father be the one doing it.

This time, though, it wasn't about homework.

"How would you like to observe a delivery sometime?" he asked, hand on the newel post at the foot of the stairs.

Now I was stunned, not so much because of the sudden visual there on the landing of an exposed woman, but because of the novelty of my father inviting me to do something. This was in the days long before cell phones and pagers, meaning that, as a solo practitioner he was never free to invite me places, the way my friends' fathers did them. As a result I had never learned how to respond to an invitation from him and before I could he went on: "Might be anytime. Even middle of the night. Jacket and tie, of course."

My father was a very jacket-and-tie kind of person, his starched white shirts just as crisp when he came home from the office in the evening as when he left for his rounds in the morning, and the prospect of accompanying him into the land of the "Lying-In" or "Bethesda" of his urgent phone calls was a bit unnerving. Over the following days I even had trouble getting to sleep at night, anticipating the knock on the door, the dressing under pressure. It might have helped to share my anxiety with friends, but I never quite found the opening. Witnessing brain surgery or the search for bullets in a chest would have been one thing, but a woman in the throes of childbirth? It just didn't jibe with those aspects of reproduction my

97

friends and I were more focused on at that time of our lives. And I certainly didn't feel comfortable asking my father for more details, betraying not only my anxiety but my ignorance, and so, as usual, it was my mother to whom I ended up confiding. Was I sure I wanted to see a delivery? she asked: that sort of thing wasn't for everyone. What she meant, I suspected later, after my parents divorced, was that one of the people that sort of thing wasn't for was me, not because of its blood-and-guts reality, but because it might tempt me to consider a career that she herself had come to resent.

Just what time of night it was when my father woke me, I don't know, only that the overhead light was blinding as I pulled on my clothes and tied and retied my tie. Silently, so as not to waken my mother, we went out to the car, got in, and drove off. After several more minutes of silence, my father confided a few facts about the patient, using words like multip and dilation, as if I might actually know what they meant. She had agreed to have me in the delivery room, he added, and understood that I was considering going into medicine myself. Why she would have understood that I couldn't imagine. Although my parents' friends had always asked me, as far back as I could remember, if I planned to follow in my father's footsteps, I had never, to my recollection, said that I did. Not because of the obstetrics, particularly, just the footsteps.

This obviously wasn't the time to get into that, though, and we drove on in silence. The mood in the car, as we waited for lights at empty intersections, passed shuttered shops and sputtering street lamps, progressed from serious to grim. No doubt there was a lot on my father's mind, reviewing the case and anticipating the many details that must be involved in the emergence of a new life. Yet, sitting there motionless in the passenger seat, I felt increasingly troubled by our silence, then personally responsible for it. Surely when he drove in for deliveries on his own, without me, it wasn't like this. Serious, sure, but not grim. Or was the delivery not the point this trip? Was I? Was this some kind of test, a coming-of-age rite like the ones I read about in *National Geographic*, or the Bar Mitzvah one of my classmates had had a couple of years back?

None of these questions did I dare raise either, desperate though I had become to break the silence. Asking about deliveries would be appropriate, but I didn't know enough about them to come up with a sensible question. Nor could I about hospitals, having never even been inside one before, except, I assumed, when I was delivered myself. But there had to be something I could ask or say that would show I was interested in my father's work, and appreciated his involving me in it. Whether that was actually the case or not was beside the point.

"You must have to be perfect all the time," I blurted out.

"What was that?"

"Oh, I was just thinking how a doctor must have to be... perfect. No mistakes."

What was that indeed, other than the projected insecurity of a teenaged son? As I listened to the words echo in the car I knew they had absolutely nothing to do with the life and concerns of a professional, an adult, a father. My head bowed under the weight of his certain disappointment.

"Depends on how you define them," he said. "How would you define mistakes?"

This wasn't his disappointment; it was worse: his logic. It was what often happened on those rare occasions when my father and I talked at any length. I would say something about a movie I had seen, or news I had heard on the radio, something I thought obvious and safe enough to bring up. Then he would reply by asking for definitions of the terms I was using, or the source of the assumptions I was making, none of which, of course, I had ever thought through. I should have known, stranded there with him in that car, that if I was going to bring up perfection and mistakes—especially if I was going to bring up perfection and mistakes—I should have some idea what I meant by the words. I didn't, but this time that was all right: the silence had been filled and the neon EMERGENCY was looming into view.

Now, of course, I know my question wasn't such a bad one after all. Medical errors, with all the cost and suffering they entail, are a big topic these days, and I know from my own practice that mistakes, however defined, are inevitable:

99

just as no medical student scores one hundred on every test, no doctor can be expected to make the right call every time. Indeed, I was an only child because there had been problems at my birth, some mistake, perhaps, had been made. Back there in that car did my father know I was getting at something important? Would he have told me so had our ride lasted just a few minutes longer?

We pulled into DOCTORS PARKING, got out, and walked into the hospital. The lobby was bright, empty, and, except for one overhead page, silent. Nearly silent, too, was the elevator as we rode up, making me think for a moment I might be drifting through a dream. But when we stepped out onto the obstetrical floor reality returned—people in scrubs writing at counters, talking on phones, others crisscrossing the big room with charts and equipment, greeting my father with great deference when they passed nearby. He introduced me to several, referring to me as his new assistant. They nodded and smiled knowingly: he's following in his father's footsteps.

After a hushed conversation with a nurse and a glance at a chart, he hurried me down a corridor and into a room of lockers and benches where he handed me a scrub suit, a paper hat, and shoe covers. Changed into these, we moved next door into a room of sinks and cupboards, where he showed me the scrub procedure. It seemed to take forever to lather up, scrub, brush nails, rinse, lather up again, scrub again to the point of pain, rinse again. Reddened arms raised, we dripped the water from our elbows, then dried with offered towels, and slipped into the sterile gowns held at the ready. Gloves came last, stretched open for our downward plunging fingers, then snapped smartly around our sleeves. Backing through a swinging door we entered the delivery room.

How bright it was. And there in the middle, lying supine on a narrow table in the glare of surgical lights, covered with sheets, knees cocked and spread, was the patient. My father moved to her, said a few words. She made an effort to glance, I thought, toward me, then cringed and bit her lip. A nurse guided me away, closer to the wall, as my father talked further with the patient. He kicked a wheeled stool into place and

100

squirmed into the drapery. I couldn't really make out what he was doing there between the woman's legs, but was amazed that this sort of thing was happening at all. Of course, having done a similar procedure countless times since, it's impossible for me to imagine the feelings of that long-ago innocent self.

There followed whispered conversations with a nurse, then listening with a stethoscope and the attachment of wires under the sheets. There was another examination, more words with the patient, a call by a nurse from a wall phone, while all the while I became increasingly aware of the set of my father's jaw. I knew that set from past disappointments, though certainly it had nothing to do with me this time. As far as this procedure was concerned, I might just as well have been back home under my own sheets, sound asleep. Curiosity aside, I wished I were.

Suddenly another doctor banged through the scrub room door, chased by a nurse trying to tie up the back of his gown. Gas tanks arrived, a table of gleaming instruments; IV poles were installed. The new doctor gave injections. Within seconds, it seemed, he had thrust the patient back flat on the table, forced a tube down her throat, and my father, as if he were simply drawing a line with a red marker, sliced the huge white belly in half.

The next thing I knew I was on my back. I was on a bench, my hip sore. I could see lockers and faces. Someone was holding my legs up in the air and talking to me. What they were saying I don't think I knew even back then, but eventually they let my legs down and eased me into a sitting position. They made me drink a full glass of water and then left.

Now what, I wondered? Wait there? Return to the delivery room? Would I be allowed to, now that I must have been on the floor and was no longer sterile? Would my father expect me to return? Would he be disappointed if I didn't? If I did? That I had fainted, which I must have? But what was I thinking, it finally came to me? Something much more significant than my behavior or even his expectations was at stake here.

I stayed sitting on the bench for what seemed like a very

long time, trying to imagine just what it was that had happened, but unable to get beyond the vision of that long red line. When my father finally reappeared, he looked so haggard I wasn't sure it was he at all, until he made one of his little clicks out of the side of his mouth. He said nothing, either about the delivery or me, as he proceeded to dress. I dressed as well, pacing my progress to his lest I end up with nothing to do.

"You all right?" he finally said as we headed for the door.

"Yeah, sure. I'm fine," I said. "Sorry I...."

But he was already out: enough words for now. We rode back down on the elevator, walked the long hall, the lobby, made our way out to the car, and headed home. Again we rode in silence, but a very different silence this time: one I wasn't responsible for. Rather, one I was grateful for, for my father's sake as well as my own. It gave us both a chance to think. Some crisis had obviously occurred back there, changing the wonder of a natural delivery into a surgical emergency— Caesarian section. I knew that term because I had once heard my father explain to someone its derivation from Caesar's own surgical birth. But what had gone wrong that required it? When had it, and when had my father realized it had? He must not have suspected anything when he woke me, because he certainly wouldn't have wanted me in the way in that case. Had one of the nurses told him of a complication when we first got there? Had he not realized it until he rolled in on that little stool? Realized rather, in the awful glare of that moment, that he should have gone in to the hospital earlier, examined her sooner, should have detected or at least suspected that something was going terribly wrong?

How badly I wanted to ask him these things. If there were ever a time for impressing my father with questions too apt for definitions and assumptions, this was it. Yet I didn't dare. Surely if he had considered the episode one of those, what we now call, teaching moments, he would have told me about indications for C-section, what was going on in this patient's case, maybe even about the historical derivation of the term. The fact that he didn't must have meant something bad had resulted, like the baby dying, or the mother, or both. No way was I going to put him on the spot if that might be the case.

The next day was a Saturday and when I finally got up my mother asked me about the delivery. She obviously knew I had gone with my father in the night, but not, apparently, how things had turned out. Had he confided nothing to her? Was that typical of their relationship? If I told the truth, that I thought something bad might have happened, would that betray my father? Had he confided but asked her to keep it to herself? In that case, if I lied wouldn't she know I had? In the end, I just said I didn't remember much: I'd fainted. Which I had.

All my father ever said afterwards was that he'd been forced to operate—that happened sometimes. Perhaps the episode was too painful for him to go into, or he thought the details would be too painful for me. For my part, I never brought it up because of the disappointments I sensed lurking in both of us. At any rate, the upshot of our mutual denial was that we kept our distance while at the same time sharing, if not acknowledging, the unique bond we now had.

It wasn't long after this that my parents sat me down and explained that they were separating. I couldn't help thinking that that night at the hospital, still looming so large in my mind, must have had something to do with it. Not that my mother would have left my father because he made a mistake in his work—if he had—but because of the way he dealt with it. With her. A mistake of another order of magnitude that would be. Though, as my father had said in the car en route, What are mistakes? How do you define them? Or, as I might now add, looking back through the fog of my own missteps, who gets to define them? The doer? The sufferer? A disinterested observer? A majority of the disinterested?

If a mistake was the cause of the separation, my mother, of course, could have been the one to have made it. She could have failed to give my father the support he needed that night, if, in fact, he needed some. She could have regularly failed to give him support over the preceding years, so that when he really needed it—if he did—he didn't dare turn to her.

103

As he should have dared turn to his son. But could I possibly have provided the father, to whom I still trembled to show my homework, to make an observation or pose a question, solace? If, as I had wondered in the car on the way to the hospital, the delivery was not only about a patient having a baby but about a son undergoing a rite, was my failure ever to ask the innocent question—What happened in there?—and thus provide the solace that only innocent questions can, my failure to come of age? My mistake? A mistake compounding, if not actually born of, my original mistake of asking about mistakes? Surely that question, blurted out against the silence, could not have caused what followed. How disappointed my father, my logical father, would have been to hear his young son express such superstition. Though perhaps not as disappointed, as hurt, as he would have been to hear his grown son revisit the events of that night from the safety of his own knowledge and his own innocence.

As my parents are no longer living, and old hospital records have long since been purged, despite all my medical knowledge I will never have answers to many of these questions. Tragedies happen, in delivery rooms as in marriages, and that may be all that can be said. One thing I have learned, though: Caesar may have died by the knife, but there is no good evidence that he was born by it. The obstetrical term associated with his name is a misnomer.

IN THE MOMENT

37.3° centigrade. Silence. Darkness. Serous fluid as well as blood drenching Denonvillier's fascia. Tiny bubbles of the afternoon studding the meaty walls now approximated. Clots, coagula, lymph filling residual spaces. Leukocytes, mast cells lining the margins of the neurovascular bundles, inhabiting the residual junk of cauterized collagen, muscle, fat. 2.0 Monocryl sutures holding the vesicourethral anastomosis fast against the increasing drag of tissue tension. Flaccid levator ani, pubococcygeus, puborectalis lying close to their would-be anatomical positions. The dorsal venous complex leaking still.

Thomas Babson—if that is what this physico-chemical entity, supinely disposed beneath the starched sheet of his hospital bed, qualifies at the moment as—sleeps. Or sort of sleeps. Not much sign of anything going on upstairs, anyway, except for the usual vegetative functions. There is, though, among those routines, a quirk. An aliquot of acetylcholine has just arrived in a particular synaptic cleft. Something afoot down below, it whispers in chemical-speak, something of a visceral nature, ancient, profound, egregious—threatening, in fact, to barge through the veils of modern pharmacology and into the forebrain. Into the whereabouts of the real—three hours and change ago, at least, real—Thomas Babson. Danger! Danger! Danger!

Michel Lieberman, MD, second year surgical resident, is whipped. He was in the OR from one until four in the morning with a multiple trauma, then back with Means, and still has three more post-ops to go before sign-out. Babson is in la-la land. Dressing's a bit bloody, catheter's draining, pulse one forty. Better grab a pressure. Got to be the daughter sitting

105

there. Bare, spreadable legs. Ringless. Wifey's pissed no one's answering her call, prefers watching the IV to him. Wifey just wants her man out of here. Wifey wants Means. Wifey wants Means to swish in in his long white coat and squeeze her hand and look her in the eye and tell her that that cock of hers'll be standing up and saluting in no time. But how about the rest of him?

Clepsydra. The water clock. 513 cc's Ringer's lactate left in the labeled liter bag. The drop partway down in its plastic chamber, following its gravitational vector toward the center of the earth. The pear-shaped drop that represents, as much as anything represents, the moment. That mirrors and refracts within its flawless pendant the multiplicity of the infinitesimal present. Like the ruby droplet hanging from the end of the catheter, certain to fall—mass, viscosity, surface tension inter-relating just so—into the clear bag hooked over the bed rail. Like the inchoate drop of morphine lying in wait in its tubing until that age-old notion of pain dawns over the Hollowfill pillow like the most ominous of suns, and the red button is... gropingly... sought.

On the bedside table stand three cards, agape. One is from *all the gang* at the brokerage house. It's a "Far Side." Everyone signed it and most went in as well on the elaborate flower arrangement glorious in the sunset glow of the windowsill. The middle card is from the McVanes down the street. It features a verse about healing as a mind-over-matter thing. Betty, who is known for such sentiments, but would not have meant to imply by this one that any complications, up to and including death, were evidence of a weak mind, signed it for both of them. The last is from TD. He has balanced his get-well-soon-or-else guy sentiment with rather more elusive financial apologies for not making it across country for his father's surgery. *Love ya*, he concludes.

This doctor, so-called, is grungy, unshaven as a movie star. His English.... The surgery took longer than expected—

106

they knew that—but why again? By her watch, it is 6:03 and Cheryl is weary of hospital chairs. She has been sitting here in room 3381 with her mother ever since she arrived from the airport just after noon. And they've long ago—measured in years now—run out of things to say to one another. That must be why her mother's first reaction was to call TD, like he could say something intelligent. The wait for TD to pick up has made her father look even more decrepit. Is that in fact her father lying there, pillow-pale, mouth all wrong? Is that how he really breathes, how he really sleeps? Could they have switched fathers on her, the way they switch babies and legs and reports?

Louise is disappointed, to say the least. This know-nothing in dirty whites, the slowness of the IV, Means, TD not answering, Cheryl with her attitude. But she has learned over the years to harbor multiple disappointments simultaneously in a way that yields, through a curious emotional calculus, a certain satisfaction, a certain paradoxical sense of validation. She knew surgery was not the way to go. That her husband should have done those atomic seed things, like Morris. Morris went home the same day. Morris will not need plastic on his chairs. Morris will not be packing diapers and penile pumps in his carry-on. And now here's some illegal alien who doesn't know the case, who's telling them what again? Means was not the right choice. Called her on the phone from Recovery to say, "slick as a whistle." Surgery lasting an hour longer than promised, and that's "slick as a whistle" when your underling says what again? Everybody said Hopkins for prostate. And TD—a get well card and then sit out there on the West Coast ignoring your phone? What about all those soccer games in the rain? Those nights waiting up for the tires to crunch across the gravel?

In the darkness, the *Babson, Thomas R.*, folder sandwiched between *Baar, Leonard*, and *Barber, Wesley J.* As it contains so far only the biopsy report, it is only a thin folder; yet is, like its fellows alphabetized in its file drawer and in all

the other file drawers of the Department of Surgical Pathology, wound-like. A wound—capable of opening and closing
but never healing—in the life and assumptions of at least one
individual. *Final diagnosis: (A) prostate, left, needle core biopsy: Infiltrating prostatic adenocarcinoma, Gleason Grade
3+3. Tumor involves one of four cores. (B) Prostate, right,
needle core biopsy: Infiltrating prostatic adenocarcinoma,
Gleason grade 3+3; score 6. Tumor involves one of four
cores.*

On the other side of the wall the corresponding micro-
scope slides—microns-thin sheets, lovely as rose windows, of
Thomas R. Babson—standing in narrow metal trays in their
own numbered drawers. The bloody gland itself, steeping in
formaldehyde, still slightly warmer than ambient laboratory
temperature, waits in its labeled jar on a countertop around the
corner next to a French teacher's gall bladder, a taxi driver's
gangrenous toe. Its cells, the good and the bad, are dying or
dead, though who can say if now is the moment of death of
any particular one of them? If any moment is.

Up two floors, down the nearly darkened hall, Maureen
Jacobs, ear phones in place, has paused to stare at Dr. Means'
first words on the screen before her: *After the usual skin preparation, a standard midline incision was made down to....* She
has paused because of an unusual hitch in the voice, an unusual stillness surrounding the words, but, though she has tran-
scribed his dictations for almost ten years now, and could type
out his entire radical suprapublic prostatectomy operative note
from memory, she would never take that chance. This would
be the time when something was different. When a complication occurred to vary, if by a single phrase, the familiar text,
the familiar, intimate voice in her ear. She will back up and re-
play, hoping. For him.

Travis Means, MD, caught in traffic. The bridge must be
up. He told his wife he'd be home by six thirty, but now.... He
has left the engine running for the heat, though it might be ten
minutes and that is a waste. Greenhouse gasses. They've got
to get going on that hydrogen thing. He's sixty—not exactly,

of course, as that would be an extraordinary coincidence, not to mention unknowable with any degree of confidence because when do "we" actually "begin"?—and has recently wondered if he will live to drive a hydrogen car. All around him he's aware of people waiting behind closed windows. One talking on her cell phone. Guy lighting up. He's aware as well, in the miracle of the instant, of honking. For the precious now, there was no drop in blood pressure, no anesthesiologist's sudden frown. There was no operation. No past of any kind, as far as that goes.

Although the local news has started—with a trailer fire—Diana couldn't care less. She's squinting at the wine bottle, now empty. Or one last drop. Tommy may have left another bottle in the kitchen closet. She is convinced that the pain of their separation in his hour of need, like the cancer itself, is God's punishment for her—for their—transgression. But it's not about the sex. Never was. God's got to understand that. And when Tommy comes back, he's got to understand that, too. They have so much else. She's dying to call the hospital. Say she's a cousin from out of town, just calling to check. But she knows something happened. She felt one of her shivers, which must have been when it did. She always knew that something would happen, just not what. Certainly not when.

Josh Milberg sitting at his desk holding *Fortune*, in the midst of a cringe. The lights are out everywhere else at the offices of Milberg and Babson. Although he's the senior partner, Josh is still always the first in, last out. Can't stand being with his wife, is what everybody says—he knows that. But let people think what they want, he's often thought, and partially thinks now; though it's funny how he never hears anybody say such things about Tom. It being after six—he's heard the distant tolling of the lobby chime—he knows he should leave. What he really should do is swing by the hospital on his way home and see how the poor bastard made out. Eesh! Smarts down there just to think about it.

Mrs. Florence Babson is back from the dining room. The Independent Livers eat at five, which seemed early to her when she first moved in, but not anymore. She's already settled in front of the television in her robe. The screen is dark because there's something about the news these days. It isn't like news used to be. In her lap lies the phone, handy in case Tom and Louise call. They haven't called recently, but they said they were gong to be away for a while when they called a week ago—or was it two weeks? You'd think they'd call and let her know specifics if they really were going away, if they were already away. Keep her posted. How busy can you be with no one left at home except a dog? Another two whole hours until it's time for bed. Dust on the screen. People don't know about dust anymore.

Out in San Francisco it's just after three. TD sitting in his cubicle, looking out the tinted window at a sun filtered through layers of cloud. Two hours away from having wasted another entire day of his life. But when the market's flat like this, who's going to buy? Or sell? They're all quick to blame him, yet so slow to give him credit. The suspicion that he should have stayed a high school science teacher is some element of his awareness as well. As is the suspicion that that tiny somewhere music is his cell phone. It's a gazillion degrees right now on the surface of the sun. Eight minutes ago there too, they say. Yeah, it is his phone.

ORANGE IS ALWAYS THE WAY

Today the trees are red. Yellow and orange beyond the green place. So green and smooth and flat that place. Level! Level is one that goes backwards as well as forwards. He could tell someone that. Her.

A faraway man is hitting a tiny white thing out there. It does not go away. He keeps hitting the white thing, standing over it and hitting it back and forth across the green place. Back and forth. His hands are covered so that they will be warm. You can also tell there must be a hole in the green place though you can't see it. The man has a name that has an L. Level is the one that starts and ends with L. It has to, father said. To count.

Feeling a need, he turns from the real window. On the set, people are running in the streets. That's what it always shows, and he would like to turn them off, but he can't take the time to find the turn-off thing right now. He has to hurry. As he passes, there is smoke, sirens. There will be burns. There will be weeks in the burn places, turning the black bodies from this side to that, applying moist and helpful things and hoping.

In the bathroom he strains and waits, listening to the noise that starts overhead every time he turns the light on. Beyond it, he still hears the set, people wanting you to buy things. They are beautiful, those people. They have good faces and good, long arms. They are how everyone would look if only they could.

Now he's sitting on the bed, working off one shoe, then the other. He stands to let his trousers drop. Sitting again, he takes out his money thing, his key, scraps of paper, a hard roll. Things. But it's time to get into bed, time to close his eyes, though the clock says five and that is when they want him to eat. They will call him and ask why he's not eating and not like him if he doesn't eat when it's time. He walks over to the closet and takes from a hanger another pair of pants. After a while they're on. When he stands and pulls the little thing it comes right up to the top. Up and down. Zipper! Someone thought of one once, and for the first time.

In the closet are many ties, some on the floor. Pants, too. Goodness. He takes down a tie, puts on the closest jacket, and walks back into the living room. It is darker outside now. The trees have lost all color. Sadness is all that's left, without the man and the little white thing.

And now he's looking at himself, at his own face and clothes, right there in front of him. As he flips the ends of the tie around to make the knot, he sees the lamps, the long couch, the painting. He is looking ahead, knowing they are behind him. It is easier to tie without looking. That makes no sense but it is true. He could tell her that.

He pushes the knot up against his throat, but not too tight. Nothing should be too tight there. Oh no, not there of all places.

He takes his time. Colored leaves on some doors, like outside. Orange and red berries. There are many rooms to go. He used to count the rooms, the steps, on the way to the eating place. It was all written down on pieces of paper. He could bring out the papers and show the ones he met in the halls how far everything was from everything else. People smiled. He can't remember any of it: it's all in pockets now.

MR. AND MRS. JAMES WHITMORE. MRS. FLORENCE DEMING. DR. AND MRS. RALPH R. BOWMAN. He knows them. They live the other side of their names in rooms just like his, or just the other way around, except for the things in them. He can hear some of their noise, though that doesn't mean they're home. A phone is going but no one answers: they're not home is why. MRS. CARMELITA JOHNSON is this one not home. Of course she's not: it's time to eat.

He stops to rest at the corner where the elevators are and the trash room with the barrels and the little high door for putting things to be burned up in. It's where the carpet turns from orange to blue, and where you can sit in big chairs and look all around or out. He needs to sit, but he mustn't. He supports his weight on the railing that follows every wall. He likes the orange part, his part, likes to stay there at the end of it for a minute. He would not like the blue part any more than he would the yellow. And there may be other parts, too, other colors. He's been here awhile but he hasn't been everywhere yet.

"Good evening Charlie."

"Good evening." He gives a little wave with his free hand as a couple passes. They are clean and nice, but are the ones who walk so fast, and always sit at the side of the big place to eat. He knows nothing about them, except that they need no one, though they too come from the orange part. They dress as they should. Her fingers flash as she passes, and her throat. He has something in his ear. People say it cost as much as something much bigger but that he won't turn it on.

The carpet is blue now, but the doors are the same. The doors are always the same, with the name and the little glass hole you can't see in or out either. Backwards or forwards. He has tried to look. He doesn't know who lives here. Only names do. It is too different. The blue is why it is different. They are the same way about him. He is orange and that is different to them. They know nothing about him.

"Dr. Benton. Good evening to you, sir." The woman is standing there waiting for him with her same flat thing in her hand. Her nametag isn't right; he can't read it. "Oh, let me just—there!—straighten your tie. May I seat you with someone tonight?"

The tie is tight now, the way she likes it. "Someone. Yes."

"I'm sure Mrs. Coursen and Mrs. Stern would like to have you join them." She winks at him. You can't see it under the skin but the thing that goes all around the eye is what closes and opens the eye. It's one of the beautiful things, hidden and beautiful. There's all about it in the big books.

"They've just been seated." Big flat thing in hand, she leads him among the rows of square white table tops. He nods, smiling, at the faces turning upwards like leaves before it rains. He knows the faces. He knows the ties and canes and

113

spectacles, but not as well as the chewing, the smiling, the frowning of the working faces. He moves his lips like words, like naming, until finally a big chair with arms is pulled back and he is seated in softness.

"Enjoy your meal!" someone says, somewhere.

They exchange greetings. Now that that one is gone he can loosen his tie. They ask him how he is and he asks them, together, how they are. Everyone is fine, though Mrs. Coursen's son is in the hospital thousands of miles away. Yes, he may have known that. She is very worried about him, and that may affect her appetite. It could be colitis, the doctors think. Or just something he ate. Cancer is way down the list. She says, "What would you say, Charles, as a medical man? Is that awfully serious? Colitis? They don't tell you a thing."

The woman standing there, waiting for him, has never stood there before. She has already finished with the ladies, she says. That means that he must speak. He says the first things he sees written in front of him—*Fruit cup, Garden salad with blue cheese dressing, Veal, Mashed potato*. She writes things down and disappears. He hopes for Mashed potato.

"One of my nephews had colitis," Mrs. Stern is saying. "Yes, I'm sure it was colitis. Of the bowels. He was always going to Boston. It was very hard on the family because they didn't have that much in those days—we weren't that close to their side, of course—and they had to stay in hotels. He was very courageous, though, I'll give him that, and he had to leave his work sometimes because, well, it's not dinner talk but...."

He sees her. She is sitting at a table just like his, but against the wall on the far side of the room. She and three others. You can't sit down with four: the arms of the chairs are too big. He watches her listen, turning her sweet face side to side as the talk moves invisibly about the table. He can tell from far away, without hearing a word, just how the talk moves. She is the one who turns this way and that and says little. Instead, she touches a corner of her napkin to her lips, then smoothes it out, white and still new, in her lap. She smiles up at the one who takes their plates but she doesn't turn

114

and look his way. Not with the talk still moving about.

"Are you both going to the movie tonight? *Roman Holiday?*" In her three years at Parkhurst, Mrs. Stern goes on, she has never missed a Thursday night movie in the auditorium, even though now she can hardly see the screen because of her macular. It's the wet macular, did she say?

He nods. He knows that about her macular. When she looks at him, he must shake his head. "Not going to the movie tonight."

"Oh, you always say that, Charlie," Mrs. Stern says, leaning toward him and tapping the tablecloth next to his hand with a long nail. It is very long and red and pointy, the nail, and makes a little place in the whiteness that stays. He watches it stay while he tries to listen. "I've never seen you at the movies, I don't think. Have you Elizabeth? Don't you enjoy movies, the old ones? I wouldn't give you two cents for the ones they make now, but the old ones…."

"Don't enjoy movies," he says. It's bad to do it, but he's going to keep on anyway, going to tell them something that's come before his mind so clearly that he can almost reach out and put his fingers around it. "I went with her when she went. She knew them. About them."

"That was your wife you mean, Charlie," Mrs. Coursen says. "Weren't you the perfect gentleman? Still are, I'd say." She coughs until she takes a sip of water.

None of them has dessert. Mrs. Stern wants to be sure to get her seat in the middle of the front row, which is the only place where she can make out who's who. Mrs. Coursen, whose plate is still full, can't face dessert. Not now anyway. He stands and pushes his chair in as far as he can so they can pass.

The group of four have left their table, but he can see the one he wants standing out by the tree in its thing near the thing that goes up and down. He makes his way past all the chairs, nodding again, this way and that, though there are fewer to nod to now. She is standing alone, holding her small shiny black thing in one hand and looking at nothing. Sometimes she stands like that for a long time. Looking.

115

"Yes?" he says when he gets close enough to her. "Yes."

"Charles. How nice to see you. Did you just finish?"

"Yes." When he breathes in there are flowers.

"I'm just standing here trying to decide about the movie. Such momentous decisions we have here at Parkhurst."

"Yes. About the movie. At Parkhurst."

"You know, I don't even know the name of the movie. Isn't that silly?"

"Silly. Yes. No!" She has the best skin of all of them. The best nose and eyes and lips that thin to a dearness when she smiles, like now. He could touch them, but not make them better. "I have that."

"And what's that you have, Charles? Another of your puzzles, I hope?"

"Yes." He reaches into one place in his jacket after another, his trousers. He can't remember now if this is where it is. It could be far away. His fingertips come to crumbs, a paper. He checks the words, to be sure: EGAD! A BASE TONE DE-NOTES A BAD AGE. He smoothes it against himself to make it the best it can be for her and holds it out.

She reads it. "Oh, that's a good one. The best one yet, I think. You're so clever, Charles. You really are, you know. Cleverest one here, I'd say. By a long shot."

He shakes his head. "I don't make. That go...." He makes a back-and-forth with his hand.

She smiles up at him as she gives the paper back. "I think I've decided it's too late for a movie. Do you think? Unless, are you going, perchance?"

"It's too late for a movie. Perchance."

"Well, I guess I'll have to just wish you a good night then, Charles."

He watches her walk over to the elevator. She doesn't walk right, but even that about her is good. When she steps inside she turns under the light, still smiling. As the doors close in from the sides, her hand rises. It waves until it's gone.

Since she leaves that way she does not live where he lives, where you just walk until you come to the place to eat, and then back when you're done. The carpet he is walking on

116

now is red both ways, forwards and backwards. He stops under a light, takes out the thing from his pocket, and goes through papers until he finds the right one, the one folded twice. KATHERINE. That's it! That's always it when he comes to the right paper. But he has never been to her part. He does not know how to get there. He does not even know her color. He is orange and wonders now how to get back to orange, but that means nothing. If you keep walking, you get everywhere. You have to. You can always go up and down as well as back and forth. It's all together here. Finally you will come to your own door, or to a door that says that one on the paper.

EGAD! A BASE TONE DENOTES A BAD AGE. It works both ways each time. Lots of things work but only a few both ways. He worries whether she really saw about that. Whether he should have begun to tell all he knows.

She is nowhere. He walks on, red as far as he can see both ways.

The newspaper is big; bells are ringing. It's the day they will make the food he wants. But he doesn't know when she is coming. She might have written it down for him, but he doesn't know where. All he can find written on the papers in kitchen drawers and pockets and stuck in books on the table by the pictures in black frames are his words, and KATHERINE. He doesn't need that word today, because she isn't the one coming, but he keeps finding KATHERINE anyway. And each time he reads it, KATHERINE becomes her face.

On the set, people are sitting around a table. They keep talking. They laugh and point at each other. He would like to get rid of them, but doesn't see the thing to get rid of them with.

He lies on the couch. He can't go somewhere because she might come and say why did he go somewhere? Why did he make her worry and go hunting all over the place for him? But he's missing the food that he likes.

This was always the day the one in the picture made that kind of food for him. She smiled when she set it in front of

117

him and stood there, waiting for him to begin. That was how it was then. Now is different. Now is the time to close his eyes.

Knocking and knocking and knocking.

"Caught ya napping, huh, Daddy?" She has things. She sets them down on the place in the kitchen and walks over to hug him. Her coat, her cheek are cold. "So how's tricks?"

She throws her coat over the back of a chair. They sit on the couch and she asks him about his back and his eating and is he going to Water Aerobics like she asked? She gets up as she always does to turn off the talking. She doesn't like the talking when she's there. Returning to the couch she makes her face: "Where's Mom?"

Mom. He feels bad. He is bad.

"Who would mess with Mom's picture?" She is angry. But no one messed with it. She looks under things and behind them and again and again. "Here it is! How'd it get down there in the drawer with your albums? You've still got those albums? I thought...."

He's not sure how it got down there in the drawer with the albums, but it is good that she has found it. She sets it upright on the table with the other pictures, only in the wrong place, and returns to the couch with a big box. Inside it is a coat. For winter. "Now, don't you go saying anything. You've got to be able to get out and about." She's happy.

"I don't go about," he says.

"Because you lost your coat, Daddy. That's why you don't go out. Now you've got no excuse. I'm going to sew your name and my phone number in it this time, right...." She points to the place on the inside where she will do it. "Hey, you getting hungry? How about we go out, down to the Inner Harbor to that restaurant you like? Show off the new threads."

"No. It's now."

"What's now? Brunch? When you've got a chance to go out?"

As they drive through the streets, she tells about the house with the bowling alley she's just sold for nearly a million, about the Halloween outfit she bought for Susan. She'll bring pictures next time. He watches the buildings pass, the cross

118

streets. She knows where she's going. She might live here. He doesn't think he ever did.

From their seats in the restaurant they can look out. Flags are snapping, the water is white in places. A boat passes. Other boats pitch and strain. There are only a few people out there. They walk fast, because they're late. Or cold. Or know things.

"Have I been here?"

"Of course, Daddy. I've brought you here bunches of times. Beautiful, isn't it, even this time of year?"

"Beautiful this time."

He has the pancakes with syrup he wants. She feels more like lunch. She asks him about the people on his floor. She knows every one of their names, all their numbers, but there's nothing he can say about them for sure. One of them might be dead now. He eats among them, but no one speaks.

She makes her face. "No one speaks? Go on. You just don't pay attention to what they say, Daddy. You've got to *attend*."

He nods. He's not hungry now. It's over. "I have one," he says. He pats his jacket.

"You and your palindromes. But they're good for the brain, they say. All those wordy things are."

He may not have it. He feels everywhere and then takes out tissue and papers from his wallet. She touches his arm. "Who's Katherine?" she asks, pointing to the name on one of the slips she has unfolded.

He looks up. His heart is missing. Katherine. But, oh no, her paper is all sticky now.

"Someone at Parkhurst? The nice lady in the bank office?"

"Yes," he says. "The lady." He tries to wipe off the syrup with his finger, then folds the paper and works it back in where it was. It doesn't go right.

She pays, helps him into his coat, and they walk outside. She holds his arm. The wind is strong, cold, but he has a coat and it is a good one. It's heavy and black and soft against his chin.

119

In the car she asks him if he needs to stop anywhere on the way home. Does he need shaving cream? Sweeties for the evening?

His fingers stick together. There's nowhere to put them.

He tells her he needs nothing.

Victoria! That's her name.

The man behind the counter says he has lived in Baltimore all his life, and that he hasn't seen snow this early in the season since he was this high.

He himself knows about snow. To get to the ones who need him, he has pushed it away many times. He always had things for that with him. He knows that snow has never kept him from fixing people. Snow must never do that. Nothing should, for that matter, father said.

"Do you...?" he asks the man when he has stopped talking about Baltimore and snow. He holds out a paper.

"Katherine? I used to date a Katherine...just kidding. You mean here at Parkhurst. She a resident?"

He nods, feeling the smile rise through his cheeks. Resident. That's what he was once before too. In a very big and special place to wear white in.

"Well, there's Catherine Mellon, Mrs. Mellon, but she's with a C. You mean Katherine Enders, I'll bet—pretty, kind of limps?"

Katherine Enders is the right one. He can tell from what it does inside him. "Yes. Katherine Enders and... where."

"You mean her apartment number. 437. You're all the same address here, you know." He writes something, hands the paper back, and then someone is calling after him, "Hey! Dr. Benton! Don't forget your album!"

He steps out when the 4 lights up. He walks along green carpets, checking the numbers on each door. 411, 413, 415. 437 is what the paper says, so he keeps going, occasionally passing people. He might know them. They smile and nod, moving over toward the railing as if he were too wide. He knows they wonder what he's doing walking on green. If he's wrong.

120

451. He is on yellow now, and the number is too big. He turns and walks back, stopping to look at each door to make sure. When he comes to 437, he puts his paper back in his pocket. He moves his tie to make it better. MRS. HERMAN W. ENDERS. He knocks with the knocker. He needs to....

"Why, hello." It's her, holding the door part way open. Part way closed. She has nothing on her face. She's good that way.

"Why hello." He pushes in past her.

It is hot and smells good. The rug is deeper than his, but he can tell the walls and doors and windows are the same. He gets to the bathroom where the noise starts up with the light just like his. He puts what he's carrying on the sink, opens his pants and stands at the toilet. Nothing happens. He flushes, to make it sound right, washes his hands, and dries them on his jacket. He mustn't touch her things. They are too good to touch. On his way back to the living room, he sees her bed, just where his is. It is big enough for two, but has many pillows. They would have to take them off and put them somewhere to get in.

He holds out what he has.

"What a nice book, Charles. Is it some of your fun puzzles?"

"No fun puzzles. No fun."

Instead of taking it she leads him to the couch. They sit down.

"May I offer you some juice, Charles?" she asks. "I often take juice in the afternoon. A little pick-me-up, you know."

"I know. No."

She looks around, then back. "My apartment's due for cleaning tomorrow. I hope you don't mind."

"I don't mind. She does."

"Who's that, Charles? Your daughter? I think I've seen your daughter with you at dinner sometimes. With the short hair? She's very pretty. Takes after her mother, I'll bet."

"Yes. No."

She smiles, and finally points. "Shall I look at your book now, Charles?"

121

He grips it with both hands, keeping it and giving it at the same time. "She says no."

"Who says no? Your daughter? Why would she say no, for goodness sake?"

"Bad."

"My, my! I can't believe you'd ever have anything bad. You of all people, Charles. Of all people."

"I did it."

Carefully, without touching him, she takes the album and positions it on her lap. She smiles at him in a way that, around the eyes, is both a smile and not.

He hasn't opened his book for a long time, but as she turns the first pages he can see the faces. He knows them, even the wrong way. He knows them better than he knows anyone else. The undeveloped chins. The harelips. The hooked and angled noses, the noses missing altogether leaving dark, running holes in the middle of the once faces. The crude ears and raw eye sockets. The charred, staring flesh. And on the opposite page, what he made. The smiles, the symmetry, the smooth skin, the person once more. Joey was one. Marsha. Miguel. The taxi driver. The one who gave him deer meat every fall though he never liked it.

But already she's closing it.

"Bad," he says, the badness taking over now.

"No, Charles, no. Good. It's just I've always been squeamish. I'm one of those ridiculous people who faint. I would have been a nurse otherwise. I always wanted to be a nurse. Maybe, who knows, I could have been your nurse."

He takes it from her and stands.

"Wouldn't you like to stay? I can't offer you much—I don't cook anymore—but I can make you coffee. It's only three. Two hours yet until our dinner."

The book is heavier than ever in his hands, the room hotter. "Yes. No." He goes to the door and opens it.

"You did wonderful work," she says behind him as he leaves. "I can tell that from what I saw. Those poor people. You gave them.... Why your daughter doesn't want you to...." And then she is calling from a great distance, "Charles!

Shouldn't you be going the other way? Toward the elevators?"

It is good in the sun. You can watch who passes or comes to throw things away. You can look up and down the hall and watch. And you can turn and look outside at who is coming and going, in and out. He often knows them. They walk back and forth down below. But there are no leaves up above. It's all bare now. Bare and then blue above everything.

What he sits in is good, but it makes a place in his back. He turns this way and that until it is better. It is warm. He can close his eyes.

"Mornin', Dr. Benton." It is a woman pulling what she always does. "You got yourself a good book there?"

"Yes. No."

"Well, you better pay attention then, don'tcha think?"

She goes until she turns and is gone. She has something to do. He does too. He stands slowly and walks across the hall. The room is small and neat. It is always the same. PAPER. CANS. PLASTIC. A red wagon, just like his once, stands ready in a corner. Its long handle is angled backward. Someone has done that so someone else doesn't fall.

He strains to pull back the little door. It is high and it is strong. This kind of door must always be that way. But it is hard to hold it with just one hand and work what he has up over the top edge with the other. When it is up there things are easier. It can rest there and go either way, but, uh oh, there is only one way now. He lets go and hears it all the way down and down and down. There is a way to know how far down from the time it takes. His father did it leaning over and dropping things and listening. One thousand one, one thousand two, one thousand.....

The door pulls itself closed with a thump. He goes back out into the hall. He looks one way and the other. Orange, blue. For him, though, orange is always the way.

SO MANY WAYS TO ERR

"Put the machine down. Just think about it."

The girl laid the calculator on the table. Philip steered it around the clipboard, well out of the way. As he waited for her response, peals of hall talk, words too distant, or juvenile, for him to catch, reached the library. She tucked a strand of hair under her headscarf and bowed her head lower.

"How old each child is," he enunciated. "That's what they're after. Carl is four years older than Mary, right? Mary is three years older than Sally. So we'll write that down in algebra terms—sort of translate English into algebra? 'Algebra' comes from Arabic, you know. Your Arabic."

He'd read that downcast eyes weren't shame or shyness but a cultural thing—he was an unrelated male after all, white, not to mention an elder by a good fifty years—but would a glance kill her?

"So we'll let C stand for Carl, and M for Mary. With me?"

"Yes, mister. I with you."

"Great. So how are we going to write an equation that says Carl is four years older than Mary? Using C and M."

Her forehead wrinkled as she stole a peak at the calculator. She tapped her lower lip with the end of her pencil.

He cleared his throat. "In other words, the difference in their ages is four years. We show difference in math, in algebra, by...?"

A pause; a pencil line in the air before her.

"Exactly! Minus. Very good, Fatima." He leaned in closer, just touching her shoulder. "Go ahead. Write it down. That's our first equation."

Ruth Ann from the Volunteer office had told Philip about

125

Fatima's algebra course; before returning to the parking garage he stopped by the classroom for a copy of the textbook. As he drove out of town, he propped the volume open against the steering wheel and leafed through a few pages whenever traffic slowed. Pretty familiar stuff, it looked like, even after all the years. What had he been so worried about?

At the IGA he picked out a week's worth of frozen dinners, a bag of Iams Active Maturity dog food, pistachio ice cream, and toothpaste. Mid-afternoon had turned out to be the best time for grocery shopping: less chance of running into old patients, not to mention Jeannette's old friends, most of whose names failed him. But this afternoon, beyond the corn bin, he recognized a woman with short-cropped, highlighted hair studying the stats on the side of a jar—his former colleague Tom's wife. Her name didn't fail him, but he still headed for check out.

"Philip!"

He turned.

"Thought it was you."

"Millie. How are you?"

"Good, Philip. Question is, how are *you*? Tom was just saying, time we had you over again. Look at you, poor thing—frozen dinners."

"Too busy to cook, you know."

"I'm sure, Philip, I'm sure. Tom does say, though, he sees you at the hospital."

"Oh, yes. Record Room. Still got my project."

"Good for you. Projects are good."

"Plus some tutoring. Portland High."

"Well, then. Guess you *are* busy."

Philip smiled as he nodded, though they'd reached the conversational node he had come to dread—the moment when the niceties had run their course, and his interlocutor must be wondering whether, a year on, a Jeannette reference would be thoughtful or not.

"You're gong to have to excuse me, Millie. Got these frozen...."

"Of course, Philip, of course. But I'm calling you about

126

dinner. Someone I want you to meet."

When Philip got home, Quick was at the door, tail switching, eyes flashing above the tennis ball in his mouth. Philip put the shopping bag down on the kitchen counter and turned off CNN, Quick's social life when Philip wasn't.

"Hang on, pal. Got to put our stuff away."

From the day nine years before when she had brought the little terrier home from the animal shelter, Quick had been Jeannette's pet. She it was who had endured the puppy teeth, the obedience classes, cleaned up the early accidents. She it was who, two and three times a day, no matter the weather or season, had walked him the quarter mile to the beach, thrown sticks and balls for him to retrieve, kept his rabies and heart worm up to date. And evenings it was she who had made room for him on the couch or the glider, patted the cushion to invite him up beside her. Indeed, over those nine years, Philip suspected, Quick had spent more intimate time with Jeannette than he had himself, right up to that last vigil beneath her dangling feet.

"Okay, okay." Groceries put away, Philip got the leash from the kitchen closet. He hooked it to Quick's collar and followed him, ball still clamped in his mouth, out the front door.

All was quiet in the neighborhood. Quick, panting hoarsely, pulled Philip past the gabled houses set far back on their sloping lawns, past the wide driveways and stands of birch and maple. It was still too early for the orthodontists, the lawyers, the brokers, the executives to be returning home from downtown, and the children would be off at their practices or curled up in their finished basements with their earbuds and video games.

The cove's beach, too, was deserted, even by the tide, and, thanks to the Indian summer heat, smelled of sea mud and decaying kelp. Philip bent down to detach the leash. He worked the ball from Quick's teeth and threw it as far as he could across the shingle. Quick scrambled after it, catching up and grabbing it before it died among the pebbles. When he

127

returned it, Philip threw it again; but this time the dog, picking up a scent, perhaps, or the scuffle of a bird, veered off into the tall grass that separated shore from woods.

Philip sat down on the driftwood that dominated the near end of the beach. Silvered and worn by years of exposure, the huge log suggested, the family had always said, something monstrous, prehistoric. Among its gnarled limbs all three children had learned to climb and balance and hang, sat for picnics, carved initials, posed for family photographs. And it was here that Jeannette, once Kerry, their youngest, had reached school age, had set up the portable French easel he had given her, and tried so desperately to paint.

"Quick!" Philip shouted. A distant tuft of grass quivered. "Not too far!"

He lay back on the smooth wood and closed his eyes. The only sound was the rhythmic soft-shoe of the surf, the occasional squeal of a gull. Should have brought the algebra book with him, he thought as he let himself relax. Clipboard and pencil. Put the time to good use as well as give himself a little nostalgia rush. Though he had never let on to his classmates back in junior high, he had always loved math, loved X. In fact, it was something about X, the defiance and promise of the unknown, that had seduced him into science in the first place. Perhaps it could have the same effect on Fatima....

His shoulder blade was aching. He twisted slightly, almost falling from his hard bed, then finally stood. He'd actually slept: already fingers of shadow were reaching the water's edge; a sea breeze was picking up. Though Quick was nowhere to be seen, he would hear the crunch of footsteps and know it was time to head back: Jeannette had trained him well.

He arrived in the library ten minutes early. The table they had used before was occupied by three girls huddled over a phone, so he picked a desk in the corner, in full view of the doorway. Seated, he arranged his clipboard and pencil before him, and opened the algebra book to the section on two unknowns. *George has five dollars more than his little brother....* What did the students scattered around the big, high-ceilinged room think of him? Held back half a century? Homeless? America's Most Wanted? Or did kids even notice the real world anymore?

The bell sounded, clanging through the old hallways like a tocsin. The three girls got up from their table and, muffling giggles, left the room. The librarian at the main desk scowled at her terminal.

Five more minutes went by. Maybe Fatima was reviewing something with her last teacher; maybe she was in the bathroom. Or praying. Many of them did that, Ruth Ann had said. The school had even set aside a special room for it, to accommodate all the new Muslim immigrants.

A girl in a head scarf entered. She paid him no attention as she hurried by: not Fatima. He waited another ten minutes, trying to concentrate on George and his brother's finances. Finally he closed the book, gathered his things, and left the library.

"Didn't show," he said to Ruth Ann as he entered her office.

"I'm afraid this does happen. Don't take it personally."

"On no. Course not. She even here today?"

"Far as I know." Ruth Ann hit a few keys, scrolled through lists on her screen. "Yep. Yep. Could have forgotten. Willing to give her another shot?"

Philip wasn't sure. He'd set aside the time—not that since retiring he didn't have plenty to set aside—driven four miles into town, navigated the parking garage twice to find a place, climbed three flights, waited. Not to mention advertised to people like Millie that, "I'm tutoring." Yet what was all of that compared to a young woman's escape from Somalia, her years in refugee camps? What gave him the right, all things considered, to take umbrage?

"Sure," he said. "Of course. Tell her I'll be here next week, same time. Or another time if that works better."

"Deal."

As he left the building, he scanned the crowds of students milling about the halls and spilling over onto the long flight of steps leading down to the street. The baggy pants, the slouch-

129

es, the skin shades, phones and headsets, were hard to reconcile with his own memories of high school. Not to mention those headscarves, under one of which Fatima might well be hiding. But realizing he didn't remember her face all that well, he hurried on his way.

Rachel, the record room clerk, had worked in medical records for over twenty years, since before Philip, Jeannette, and their first two children had moved to Portland, and was usually the one who pulled his Medical Errors charts. From the beginning of his study almost three years ago, she had seemed genuinely interested in it. Was he reaching any conclusions? she asked more often now. Don't forget: you promised to show me your report when it's done.

"All ready for you, Dr. March. Couldn't find two early ones, but we're still looking. Coffee?"

"That'd be great, Rachel. Thank you. How you been?"

"Very good. And you? You're tan."

"This weather. Can you believe it?"

He sat down at the desk where his charts were piled in two neat stacks. The hospital was in the process of computerizing its medical records, but some of the charts he was interested in went back decades: it was likely they'd be warehoused and never get scanned into the system. All the more important, then, for him to analyze them now in support of his thesis that medical errors are becoming more, not less, common as medicine advances.

Heart attacks, pulmonary emboli, sepsis, strokes—so much is known about the ways to die, and yet five to ten percent of the time, he estimated, the doctors get it wrong. Of course, you still don't know that things would have turned out differently if they'd gotten it right. That would take a whole other study.

The third chart down was an overdose case, finally diagnosed two weeks postmortem when the toxicology screen came back. Not even suspected by the residents, the attending physician, consultants. Encephalitis, one had thought, closed head injury another. VOODOO?? someone had printed anon-

130

ymously.

"Hope it's not too strong for you."

"I need all the strength I can get, Rachel. Thank you so much."

He took a sip from the Styrofoam cup and placed it on the floor—coffee spills had a way of finding and blurring the most crucial entries in charts. Although that might not be such a bad outcome for this chart. He wasn't sure he wanted to read through the medical student's history where clues might be encoded in the close, obsessive penmanship—poor sleep noticed by the wife perhaps, loss of weight recorded but not questioned in the clinic record, the mention by neighbors, dutifully included by the student and just as dutifully ignored by superiors, that the patient hadn't watched the playoffs he'd always loved. The stuff of error.

"Tough one?"

Philip jumped at the voice, almost kicking his coffee.

"Oh, Tom. Scared me."

"Sorry about that, Phil. Mind?" The new arrival sat down in the next carrel, removed the stethoscope draped around his neck, and coiled it at the back of the desk. "So, how goes the research? Finding all my mistakes?"

"Errors, Tom—I don't do 'mistakes.' But slow. I keep realizing I need more cases. For statistical significance. Or probably should have kept to one disease."

"Yeah, keep it simple. My motto. And you?"

"What?"

"You hangin' in there?"

Rachel arrived with an armload of charts for Tom's signature. As Tom opened at the first tab he said, "We haven't forgotten you, you know, Millie and I."

"I'm sure you haven't, Tom. I'm fine, though, really. She doesn't have to...."

"Of course she doesn't *have* to. Wants to. We want to. Hear all about this tutoring she said? I remember you and your bedside teaching. You know you could still... oop."

Tom reached for the cell phone on his belt. He rose slowly as he listened to the call, then stepped away toward the window. Philip watched his friend talking, gesturing, tipping his head back in private laughter. He stood up himself. He bent over to pick up his cup, then walked to the front of the room where Rachel was loading paper into the copier.

"Just remembered an appointment. You can leave my charts where they are. Coffee hit the spot by the way."

Quick jerked the leash and tried to bark around the sandy ball in his mouth—he'd heard the ringing first. Philip worked the key in the lock and reached the kitchen phone just as the beep began.

"Hello?" he gasped.

"You all right, Dad? It's me."

One-handed he detached Quick's leash as he talked. "I'm fine, Kerry. I'm fine. Whew! Catch my breath. Little beach work."

Kerry had moved to Paris—the bank had transferred her was how she always put it—six months before, just six months after her mother's death. Though, or because, the most distant geographically of his three children, she was the one who called and e-mailed the most.

"How *is* Quick?"

"He's good. Energizer dog. Say hello?"

"Woof, woof."

Philip held the phone down to Quick, who cocked his head, dropped his ball, and sneezed.

"He says he misses you."

"I miss him too. Both of you. And you know what? Why I called is I'm coming home."

"No problem is there?" He pulled out the chair by the kitchen table but didn't sit.

"No, no—nothing like that. Visit. They're paying my flight, too. Any time good/bad at your end?"

"All good. Got my tutoring, but that's flexible."

"Great. Probably first of October. How's that going anyway, the tutoring? He getting it?"

"She. And yes. Bright girl, I think. Love to see her make it."

"Sure she will. So, I'll let you know, OK?"

"Can't wait. Love you."

"You too, Dad. *Au revoir*. Woof."

Philip set the receiver back in its cradle. He hung up the leash on its hook, ran the water cold, and filled the dog dish. He watched Quick take a few sloppy licks, then wander, muzzle dripping, past the refrigerator to his bed. Four o'clock by the microwave: too early to eat, he'd stalled on the Adams biography.

"Come on, Pal. Company's coming."

Philip hadn't been upstairs since the day he'd found his wife hanging through the trapdoor in the ceiling of the guest room closet. The living room couch had become his bed ever since; he'd bought all new clothes, shoes, towels, toiletries, even blankets and sheets—everything he needed for ground-floor life. Quick was the one who had gone back up, to see, Philip was sure, if his mistress might descend from the attic. Philip couldn't bring himself to go up after him, and assumed the dog would, like Greyfriars Bobby, keep his vigil until he died as well. But finally, twelve hours later, Quick trotted down the steps and barked to go out. As far as Philip knew, he had never returned either.

"Come on, Quick." Philip called from the landing. "We gotta do this, you know." He slapped his thigh several times, but all the dog did, sitting at the foot of the stairs, was bow down to nibble a paw.

Because it was late afternoon, the sunlight was nearly level, spread like butter down the carpeted hall, incandescent in the western rooms. Master bedroom, Melissa's room, bathroom, Harry's room with the chin-up bar still in place, Kerry's room. And at the far end of the hall, door closed, the guest room.

Studio, Jeannette began calling it, when Melissa and then Harry moved out, and she decided to give painting another shot. Winslow Homer light there, she said, and Philip was relieved to have something to give her again—easels, canvases, frames, pigments ordered from Provence—something that might compensate for vanishing children and a husband increasingly occupied at the hospital. But when Kerry graduated from college and moved to Boston for her teller job, Jeannette stopped going to her studio. First she said color just didn't do it for her anymore. Then that she should be spending her money on Oxfam, not art supplies. Then that she had no talent, had always been, literally, a "guest" in the arts. If she had talent, Philip, or the children, her friend Millie, someone at least would have shown a little excitement. What you need is a proper studio, Philip had countered. To physically go to. I'll find you one. There—that's excitement.

He stepped into Kerry's room. It looked as it always had—Impressionist posters on the walls; desk he had assembled when she was twelve; shelves of Pooh, Douglas Adams, French; single bed left unmade since that last touch-base before Paris. Unlike her father—or their dog—Kerry had never had qualms about the upstairs, about sleeping down the hall from a trap door.

Dust there was for sure, in the last tangents of light, covering the desk top, the bureau, the sill, with its own history. He would have to get rags, the vacuum and attachments—freshen up the room, make up the bed. Maybe even wash the window.

But he had done enough for one day. More than enough.

Philip didn't think he had ever met Beverly before—he would have remembered the intent, almost exophthalmic eyes, the powdered nevus on the left cheek—but as Millie told how, like Jeannette, Beverly had served on the art school board, in fact had gone back to it after her husband's death in a sailing accident, he began to make connections.

"It took me a good two years," Beverly was saying, "to, you know, put Humpty together again."

She was sitting in the easy chair angled next to his. Across the coffee table laden with dip, cheeses, smoked salmon, the four wineglasses, Tom and Millie had taken the couch.

"Having a schedule," Millie observed. "Very key."

"Yes," Philip said. "I maybe shouldn't have retired when I did. State of shock I guess. Like anybody. But I keep myself busy. Try to."

Tom held out the crackers in one hand, the square platter of salmon in the other. "Have some more omega-3's, Philip."

"*You* could join the board," Beverly said as Philip maneuvered the crumbly fish onto a cracker. "We could use a doctor."

"Nobody sick, I hope."

"No, no. The perspective of, I mean. Objectivity."

"Well yes, I'd consider that." He angled his hors d'oeuvre into his mouth.

"Sort of honor your wife, too."

Philip nodded, humming agreement as he chewed.

Beverly went on, "That was a wonderful studio you got her, by the way."

"You saw it?" Philip asked.

"Beverly, I...." Millie's face contorted slightly as she glanced down at the empty glass in her hand. "...I don't know if talking about...."

"It's all right," Philip said, hoping it would be. "Open is good. And it *was* a nice studio, Beverly. You're right. She loved it. At least she said she loved it. Didn't get there myself all that much, but I know she put in a lot of hours there."

"Whatever happened to her work?" Tom asked. "Her paintings? I ever see her paintings?"

Though he wasn't looking at Philip, Philip felt the thrust of the question. "That's what was funny. She talked about 'works in progress' she called them. But I didn't want to force the issue."

"No," Beverly said. "Course you didn't."

"You know," Millie said, "if we're talking about Jeannette, which I guess we are, and I'm not saying we should be or shouldn't be, I really don't think it was about her art at that point."

"At what point we talking?" Tom asked.

"When Phil got her the studio. She had it all outfitted and everything, decorated to the nines, but where it was, with other studios around, near the art school and all, she seemed more interested in the other artists, the students, the, I don't know, buzz? Than... paint."

135

"Or than the studio even," Beverly said. "Yes, I think you're right. The whole scene, really. There was that one student she talked about—remember?—that girl from up in the county somewhere, I think. Indian name. Really talented, she thought. But kind of, wouldn't you say...."

"She was devastated, I think," Millie said, "when she flunked out. Jeannette was, I mean, when the girl did."

"When was all this?" Tom asked. "Where was I?" Then, "More anybody? We're going to be eating this stuff for weeks."

In the distance a soft chime began.

Millie stood. "I'm being paged. Be about five more minutes."

Beverly set her glass down on the table and made to stand up. "Let me help you."

"No, no. You stay right there. Keep an eye on these two."

When Millie had left the room, Philip repeated his friend's question. "Yes, when was that I wonder? With the girl? You mentioned."

Beverly blinked her large eyes twice. "I'm not exactly sure, to tell you the truth. Time's a funny thing."

"Mill!" Tom shouted. "Question!"

In a moment Millie, aproned and gripping a bottle of red wine by the neck, appeared at the doorway.

"When did the Indian leave?"

Millie glanced at Philip, then looked back to her husband, her eyes narrowing. "Native American, Tom. And why would I know?"

He shrugged as she raised the wine bottle toward him. "This need to breathe?"

It was cooler in the parking garage than on the street; Philip wasn't worried about leaving Quick for an hour. Jeannette must have done it often, when she ran errands. He cracked all four windows an inch—enough for air but not an arm—gave the dog a vigorous pat on the head, and, book and clipboard in hand, headed off for the school.

In the library, he took one of the larger tables near the

136

door, put his clipboard aside, and opened the text book. As he did so, the bell, an even more urgent clangor than before, it seemed, startled him. Moments later he could hear the scuffle of feet, the familiar Babel in the hall. He leafed through the book, looking up each time he heard the library door swing open. Pairs and groups of students entered, settled at tables or in the adjacent computer room. Shortly the bell sounded again, leaving a vast, institutional hush.

No Fatima. He glanced over toward the main desk, just avoiding the librarian's eye. Ten minutes he would give the girl.

In addition to blank sheets, his clipboard still held his most recent medical error data. He looked through the columns of numbers he had produced, looking for that elusive pattern, that unifying theme, that would make sense of the senseless. Sometimes the right question wasn't asked, sometimes it was but the answer wasn't acknowledged or pursued. Sometimes the physical examination was incomplete or the obvious test wasn't ordered. Ordered but never acted on. So many ways to err.

He returned to the algebra book, for the librarian's benefit more than his own, and before the ten minutes had passed, left the library.

"Oh, she was just here," Ruth Ann said, standing from her desk as Philip entered the office. "Didn't call you?"

"No."

"That's terrible. Had a dentist appointment."

"A dentist appointment? She would have known about that."

"I'm sure she did. You or I would have called, but...."

"That's the second time."

"I'm well aware. If you've had enough I certainly understand."

"That's just it, though. I haven't."

Ruth Ann leaned back against her desk and crossed her arms. When clarification didn't come, she went on. "Tell you what, Dr. March. After midterms the really motivated kids will start coming in. I'm sure I can find a good match for you

137

then. How's that sound?"

But he was already out the door. He pushed through a crowd of boys standing on the front landing and took the steps on the diagonal, two at a time. A car honked as he started across the street. He jumped back to the curb and it was only then that he saw her standing at the bus stop—headscarf, book bag, quick dark glance.

"Fatima!" he shouted, hurrying toward her. "Why didn't you call me?"

She kept looking down. "I have dentist."

"I know that. Now. Now's too late. Should have called me. Simple decency."

She looked up cautiously. "Decency."

"Yeah, you know decency. Considering the other person."

A city bus pulled up to the stop, its doors folding back. Fatima turned toward it, but Philip had her by the shoulders, his book and clipboard clattering to the pavement as he wheeled her to him.

"Damn it, Fatima! Why didn't you tell them to call me? I drove all the way in here, a dog in the car.... To help you. I'm trying to *help* you."

She tried to squirm away but Philip gripped her more tightly, dislodging her scarf as he shook her. "Answer me, damn it! Don't you care?"

Suddenly hands jerked him back—the boys from the landing.

"What you doin' dude? You crazy? Let her go!"

Freed, she ran to the front of the bus, paused to arrange her scarf, and climbed up. The doors closed behind her bag; the bus moved away.

The hands released. The boys stepped back in a circle. He knelt to pick up the algebra book and gather loose papers.

"You don't understand," he said, back on his feet. "Believe me. I was just.... I mean, we were...."

But the more starts he made, the more the boys frowned and cocked their heads until, one by one, they turned and made their way back along the sidewalk toward the school.

VISITING HOURS

Might she herself be the dead one? Unlikely, as someone is talking to her, about Milton's golf clubs, is it? Borrowing them once? She can't follow. Not with her own question asking itself over and over again. The answer, of course, lies behind her, beneath the huge and gleaming lid of the casket: Milton in his sport coat, his birthday tie, his glasses (they had found the glasses at the hospital, cleaned them as if that mattered and put them in place). He's all dressed in there in the dark. He's ready, and though it's odd to be dressed and ready and supine in the dark all at the same time, something about him, more than about her, definitely *is*.

Perhaps that's what grief is—failure. To survive the other.

"I had no idea, Anne...." It's Sally now, from across the street. Sally and Bob. Bob's not actually there, but Sally still comes across as Sally and Bob. The wrong mail, the wave backing out of the driveway, that chisel never returned. The whole history converges in the person of Sally, in her amazement and effort and bit of rouge smeared on her left cheek. "I just saw him mowing the lawn, when, Saturday, wasn't it?"

"Yes," Anne says. She's following now, her comprehension so exquisite it's almost 3-D. "It was sudden. Grabbed his head, fell over. Thank God I was there not that."

"Wasn't the cancer, then. I thought...."

"Oh, no. But you would. Think that."

"Not that it matters."

"No, not now. Brain hemorrhage." She's drowning in the word, the blood of the word filling her own head, welling, pressing outward and down into her throat, gurgling. She coughs. "Though it would have been. One day. He'd just started new chemo. Some spots. They called them. They saw."

"Well, Bob and I—he wanted to come but.... If we can

139

do...."

"Yes, Sally, I understand. Thank you so much. And Bob."

Huh. Stroke, Sally thinks as she moves away, Bob filling her mind, his tiny blood pressure pills, how red his face gets when he is angry, which he never used to get before retirement. Or not angry—impatient is more like it. That day in traffic. Couldn't face standing around in a room with a box, he said. Box. Well, it is a box. And he could be collapsed right now on the couch, remote in hand, ball game proceeding perfectly well without him.

She sees the way out past the lilies and the red Exit sign, sees her car, all the turns. The front hall floorboard squeaks like her voice trying to scream his name.

But she's not leaving. She's not that way. She's moving toward the refreshment table where Hubert Bryce, her gynecologist, is ladling punch from a large bowl into a thimble of a glass. He has a tan and he's very good looking. Good ladling, that is.

"Hello, Sally," he says. "Punch?"

"Oh, I can.... Thank you."

"My wife, Betty," he adds, indicating the woman beside him as he hands the glass he has just filled to Sally. Sally nods toward Betty, but Betty, positioned at an angle, doesn't respond: she's talking to a young man with no hair. Sally has always wondered about her doctors' wives. Now she knows something about one of them. If only at an angle.

"Sad day," she says to Dr. Bryce.

"Yes. And more ahead of her. You knew him?"

"Oh yes. You could say. We live across the street. Lived... live. And you?"

"Hmm. Church. I was on the program committee with Milton, talked with him a little about the cancer. Quite a shock, though, open the obits and... zowie."

It occurs to Sally that she may know something he doesn't know. Something medical the doctor—her doctor—doesn't know. But she may know it in a confidential sort of context. Would she want...? "Yes. Stroke. I mean I heard."

His head moves in closer, tilted. Or the room is. "Stroke?"

140

She'll have to go on now. She gets to go on now. "Hemorrhage, his wife told me. That's a stroke isn't it?"

"Yes. Type of. Brain hemorrhage is one type of so-called stroke."

"Collapsed," she says. "At her feet. I don't know if I...."

"We're all praying for her. The family."

Betty materializes and takes her husband's arm; Sally gets one last look at her as she veers away.

"Some people have all the luck," Betty says to her husband, holding on just above the elbow.

He raises his eyebrows.

"I mean, cancer... stroke. Just started new treatment, I heard, then.... Lightning twice."

"You heard that, too?"

"Ronny. The daughter? With the, you know, partner? Said it might have been a blessing."

"Hmm." He drains his glass and reaches to set it in a clear space toward the back of the table.

Betty relaxes her grip. She won't give him up altogether, though. "What's she going to do now? That house. Never did like that house. So, I don't know...."

"Could be related."

People are still gathered as if in a line to speak to Anne. Betty knows she'll have to join them, though there's something about lines. Of late.

"The hemorrhage. I mean, I wouldn't say this to anybody, but chemo can knock out your platelets so you bleed. Including in your head. Too much chemo, anyway. Bone marrow effect. I'm not saying...."

"You gotten to her yet?"

"Anne? No. I thought we'd...."

"Oh, there's Carol. Next to the book. I've got to tell her about bridge. I'll sign us."

Betty makes her way among the groups of people nearly filling the big room. She keeps as far as she can from the end where the casket is floating darkly among the lilies. Maybe that's why she hasn't paid her respects yet. Not the line but the lilies.

141

Carol is sitting in a chair as Betty approaches, but stands on seeing her.

"Our ranks are growing," Carol says. They touch cheeks.

"At least you know what to say."

"It doesn't help, believe me. Widowness. -Hood."

"But you know her. From exercise."

Carol does a little metza-metza with her hand. "When Steven died? She spoke to me. But it's funny—next time I saw her, it was like she never had. Though what is there to say, really? Next time."

"My husband said a funny thing."

"That's my doctor."

"No, I mean.... He said the stroke...?"

"Yeah, I heard that too. Stroke."

"That his treatment could have caused it. For his cancer. Something about...."

Carol leans against the stand holding the book of condolences. Her back tires easily now. Maybe it's the exercise. Maybe bone cancer.

"Wouldn't that be awful? I mean...."

"She going to sue?"

"Oh I don't.... Hubert was just supposing. I don't think Anne...."

"Boy. That'd gall ya, all right."

"It happens, in medicine. Not perfect. Hubert says...."

Of course he does. They all would. "But if they screw up, you should know, right?"

"Well...."

"I mean, Anne should know. *Her* husband. *Her* life. Oh, she's free."

Carol withdraws though behind her Betty is saying something about bridge. When she reaches Anne, she gives her a long hug. The repeat, the reverse, the answer and cancellation of all those years ago. Five already. Going on.

"So sorry, Anne. So, so sorry. But it was quick, I understand."

Anne releases her grip and regards her friend, her fellow widow. Carol has survived. Though looks can be deceiving.

142

Up until this very moment Anne has not seriously considered the possibility that looks, in this case widows', can be deceiving. Her own now. "Good of you to come, Carol."

"Oh. You were so good to me. After Steven. Whatever you said...."

Anne looks around the room. How many. For Milton? For her? For themselves. Out of.... Will she continue to exercise, like Carol? Take exercise tights from a drawer and pull them on, one leg until it's just tight enough, then....

"You had no warning, I guess."

She looks back at the woman who still seems to be standing before her, saying things. "Warning."

"Of the stroke."

"Oh, no. Just, down he went." And there he is stretched out before her on the funeral home carpet, not behind her in the darkness under that lid where he's supposed to be. As if one place is as likely, or unlikely, as the next.

"'Cause sometimes, I've heard, chemo has side effects. On the blood."

"No. His blood was down, they said, but he never complained. He just mowed, you know, day or two before."

"I only mention it in case you want to ask the doctors or anything."

They're watching each other, people in the background, low lighting, Exit sign required by law, no doubt. Exit!

"Well," Carol says, "I won't tie you up any longer. You must be exhausted."

Anne nods but is not exhausted. She's something, clearly something, but it isn't what she would call exhausted. She watches a woman named Carol move away through the room, her hand on her back as if pushing herself forward. Now Anne is alone. She is standing alone amidst the scent of lilies. Nothing happens for what may be a very long time. She turns and walks over to a casket. Its sheen is perfect, its surface smooth to the touch, its thunder as she begins to pound, glorious.

WAR STORY

It's three. Time. Dr. Bentley leans forward, the sleeve of his robe brushing crusts from the plate onto the table as he turns off the television. He looks out the window, toward the city more memory now than perception, more fancy than memory. Carew Tower. The old Pogue's. Beyond, the wandering impression of the Ohio. Kentucky hills just woolly shadows at the foot of the sky. Far beneath him, streets and their corners where he's waited for lights. Neighborhoods where he and the gang chased and wrestled all those years ago, and he and Sarah walked, rain or shine. *Educare*: to lead, to bring. That's what his schools, the university out their somewhere did—bring him now to this living room, on this twenty-first floor, at this three o'clock in the afternoon of this October...10th isn't it?

He stands, crumbs spilling from his lap onto his bare feet. On his way past the kitchen he leaves off his glass and continues down the hall, brushing the walls, the cockeyed picture frames. In the bedroom, he lets his robe slide down over his arms to the floor and there she is again, *Je Reviens* in the air. "I'm ready."

He sits on the clothes covering the bottom of his unmade bed, and begins to work his suit pants up, one swollen leg at a time. He takes a starched white shirt from the stack on the floor, tears off the wrapper. Forget the top button—too small a space, though once upon a time he could tie double knots inside a match box. Socks. Shoes. Tie. Vest is awfully tight—all that bread and Scotch. Jacket at last.

Before he leaves, he takes from the bureau an old brown album, taped along the spine. He lays it on the top and opens it. With a few turns of the wide, brittle pages, he finds his place, and, picking up a magnifying glass, begins to study. He

145

works the glass back and forth in front of his left eye, though he doesn't need to: the scene in the photograph is already clear in his mind. Coconut palms brushing a cloudless sky. Jeep on an unpaved roadway, tents, Quonset off to the left. Standing before the jeep, smiling in their uniforms, seven people squeeze in for the shot: Tibor, their crazy chief of staff at the field hospital; Leo; Whitey; a woman he never could remember, probably a nurse; Marge, the bridge player; Bea, looking up at the sky, eyes closed, in the midst of one of her laughs; and he, Lt. Sumner Bentley (MC), USNR, the faint line of a mustache above his grin. What the picture doesn't show, but is much more obvious that what it does, is Bea's hand clasped tightly in his own.

Before he leaves the apartment, he walks into the living room. He knows, even if he can't see it, that the place is in no condition for visitors, including Raymond. Sarah would be appalled. Cartons of Scotch bottles, stacks of newspapers, bags of trash, Chinese take-out boxes, undershirts, strewn everywhere. He can feel the crunch of roaches under his feet, and stumbles, once, over a rug bunched up at the end of the divan. One of Sarah's favorite orientals, bought with a few American dollars in a Kabul bazaar. Paper-clipped to the shade on the desk lamp is a sheet of Sarah's stationery on which, months ago, he has printed in his best hand,

SON RAYMOND BENTLEY
207-787-9909.

To be sure it is obvious to whoever enters, he adjusts the sheet and turns on the light.

Down in the parking garage, he feels his way among the familiar pillars, along the smooth hoods, to 2101. He unlocks the car door and gets in.

This is always the hardest part of the day. Mornings and early afternoons, he has the anticipation of the visit, perhaps a sink bath, a bite to eat, the writing of a check under bright light, a call to the grocer. The visit itself has become more redemptive than painful as months have stretched into years.

And the aftermath back home — the pouring of the Scotch, the robe, the drone of the television — is but a prelude to the blessing of sleep. But that moment in the car, struggling to insert the key, pausing before the twist of the ignition to look out ahead through the sloping, reflective glass — that is the hardest. As a responsible citizen, a retired and once much-revered surgeon who respected the knife as much as anyone, he knows very well the danger he represents on the road. You'll always have your peripheral vision, though, Dr. Chiang reassured him last visit, but not, I'm afraid, your license.

The engine surges, idles. He's made the trip to Indian Ridge Nursing Home so many times over the past two years — daily, in fact, except during the pneumonia — that he knows he can make one more.

Rolling forward, he veers widely left, and eases toward the exit. Automatically, the great iron door rattles upward ahead of him. He moves out into general brightness, to the end of the drive, to Vine. This is the best time of day to go, he has learned. Not quite rush hour, yet the sun is low in the west. Less glare. By moving his head side to side, oscillating back and forth in quick shakes to recruit what peripheral vision he has left, he is able to create a general gestalt of the road and traffic. At the look of a break, he lunges out into the stream, maneuvering far to the right into the slow lane.

There are only two intersections between the high rise and the thruway, and once there, he sinks back into his seat, rubs his tired neck. The lane lines are fresh and bright, which helps, and he can hold around forty five. If he drifts further right there's always the breakdown lane, the shoulder, snow fences and fields. And the three massive overpass abutments between the city and his exit. He knows them well. He respects them. The only thing he really fears along the way is the sound of a siren.

Raymond has tried to help, of course, the way children do. "Come and live with us, Dad," he's said on the phone many times. "We've got the room now." Poor Raymond, thinking their leaving the city of their birth and of their life and by all rights of their death, and moving a thousand miles

147

to the Canadian woods was an option. Thinking he, Raymond, himself could have any kind of a life cloistered through those long northern winters with the blind and the mad.

He parks by the entrance. He doesn't have handicap plates—the less the state knows the better—but he knows the staff would do nothing to challenge the dedication which he represents, but which, after even two years, they know so little about.

"Good afternoon, Dr. Bentley!" a woman calls from behind the front desk. "How was the drive?"

"Not much traffic. How are you doing, Lou Anne? Jake get that job?"

"'Fraid not. Said he was over-qualified but I don't know. I'm thinkin' it's the earring."

"Yes. People so quick to judge."

"Want me to take you down?"

"I think I remember the way."

He heads across the lobby toward the corridor, the music of Lou Anne's voice floating after him: "You have a good day, now."

The Alzheimer unit is a locked one. One of the aids hears his knock and lets him in.

"Thank you, Yvonne," he calls after her.

"That you, Michael?" he asks when he reaches the nurses' station.

"We gotta get you some glasses that work, Dr. Bentley," the young man says, standing and joining him at the door. "I'm startin' to get worried about you."

"Oh, you must have better things to worry about, Michael. How's our patient today?"

"Not much change. Watching that new med. We got the poseys ready, though."

"I doubt you'll be needing any restraints for Mrs. Bentley, Michael. I doubt that very much."

"Well, you know her better'n we do, Dr. Bentley. For damn sure."

"Suppose I do, Michael. Suppose I do."

He continues on down the east wing hall, counting doorways. Sarah's room is one he'd recognize even totally blind: strains of Glenn Miller, aromas of *Je Reviens* and air freshener. One of the few private rooms at Indian Ridge, it's softly lit, and furnished with some of her favorite pieces from the old house—bird's eye maple bureau that had been her sister's, rocker with a cushion her mother had embroidered, table she had rescued from a chicken coop when he was in the Pacific. On the table stands a framed photograph of Raymond in a cowboy costume, chocolate smeared on one cheek.

"Hi there, Sweet. Sumner." He feels for the CD controls on her bedside table and turns off the music, then leans down over the bed to kiss her forehead, her cheek. He touches her face, smooth with lotion, runs his hand down over the blanket covering her shoulder, her upturned side, her bony hip. But, small and curled as a child, she continues her sleep, untroubled as a child's. He sits down in the easy chair the staff always have ready for him at the head of the bed.

"How are you, Sweetheart?" he asks, close enough to sense her warmth, her faint, stale, breath. "There's something I've come to tell you."

Who knows what thoughts stray through the debris of a mind? There must be pain perception, for there is usually withdrawal from noxious stimuli. There must be some effect of loud noise, offensive odor, disgusting taste, because we have witnessed, in the demented, reactions so like our own. But succinct ideas? Specific emotions? Coherent memories? Has the human brain been reduced in these situations to that of an animal, or worse, that awful "vegetable," its billions of exquisitely connected cells rendered no more capable of humanity than gobs of roughage in a bowl? Beneath those white hairs, behind those papery eyelids, could freak moments of sentience still spark? Could the past register, if ever so fleetingly, triggered by hands turning the body in the bed, triggered by refrains of certain music, the scent of certain perfume, the arrival of certain others? Do the daily letters, long since burned in the fireplace, ever surface in such a mind? The reunion on the front walk, flash of uniform, of polka-dots? That

149

photograph she, entering the bedroom unannounced, found him closing an album on?

Dr. Bentley does not know. Only that he must tell her. It is no longer a question of understanding. It is no longer a question of whether the past ever loses meaning. It is no longer a question of which in the end is worse, deception or hurt. It is no longer even a question of whether, like joining the war as late as '43, telling her now doesn't count for much. No, it is merely a question of conclusion.

And so he begins with the reunion on the sidewalk, the embrace, Raymond's puzzled look sucking his thumb off to the side by the flower bed. The joy he felt to be back home, the joy that, for the moment at least, eclipsed the rest. She had done so well, keeping house on her own two whole years, raising their infant son, writing daily about his progress, her longing. Writing, too, about that hospital Christmas party where everyone got drunk and his colleague Robert announced the war with the Japs was as well as won by 1943. About how those who went off then could never be the heroes that the first on the beaches were. How she had vowed never again to speak to Robert, deferred because of his hip, and who knew very well that was the year Sumner volunteered. Yes, he appreciated her defense of him, but her attitude had put him in a difficult position. He knew how badly she wanted a hero for a husband, to justify her sacrifice as well as his. But, he should tell her, Robert had been right. Her husband was no hero, operating in the tents of a secured Tulagi, taking regular R&R in New Zealand. Seeing no combat ever, only combat's toll—the torn limbs, the burns, chests full of blood, the scars Robert's real heroes would carry to their graves.

And real heroes, he goes on, don't fall in love just because love is available. But he couldn't help himself. He was a young man, and Bea—yes, that one in the picture—though not as pretty as she, not as sweetly loving, had a laugh, a fire, that she, through no fault of her own, never did. They worked together, doctor and nurse, day and night, for over six months. Sat side by side in the mess tent with the field hospital crew, wandered off down the beach at dusk, until the music from the

150

armed forces radio faded completely, and all they could hear was the slow plash of waves on sand, the rustle of palm leaves in the wind. Yes, she was with him in New Zealand. She was even there when he wrote the postcards, though she never asked to whom. And no, he never did get around to telling her he was married, a father. When she got her orders back to Seattle, they'd even promised they would find each other. He actually made that promise. He was still promising in letters to the end. If there was any consolation for her, his wife, it was that, ultimately, he had been unfaithful to Bea as well.

Oh, he continues, stroking her hair, he had been on the verge of telling her so many times over the years! But what good would it have done? Would she have thought, well, that's what heroes do, making the revelation unnecessary after all? Would she have taken the expected offense and, four-year old in tow, stormed out of his life? Or, impossible as that was to imagine, would she have stayed on in silence, plotting, and letting him know she was plotting, revenge? No matter how he tortured these questions, he could never seem to get closer to their answers, and so, postponing confrontation, he let her suspicions scar, slowly, if incompletely, the way war wounds do.

Oddly, the only person he ever did tell, and he hopes she can forgive him this, too, was Robert. It hardly matters now, of course, now that Robert is long dead, thanks to the hip that saved him from war. Some time in the sixties it was, the country slipping into yet more violence. He and Robert were waiting in their scrubs in the Surgical Lounge late one evening, and Robert, whose marriage was in trouble at the time, had asked him if he had found it hard to stay faithful during the long wartime separation. At first he had simply said, No, it hadn't; but then, suddenly sensing that he might never have another opportunity for confession, and might never find a safer confessor than a man who knew him for what he was, he went on to say he thought of it as staying faithful to two women, not unfaithful to either. He had not imagined it possible, but there it was—love on paper, and love in the flesh. He felt just as devoted when he wrote Sarah in his tent, as when he

151

led Bea down the beach.

"I had to tell you, Sweet. I've had to tell you for a long time. I love you and I always have. It's time for me to leave. But don't worry: Raymond will be here to see you before you know it."

He kisses her on her lips and stands. He watches over her still form for a few more minutes, then leaves the room, and walks slowly up the corridor toward the bright lights. No one is there at the nurses' station, as far as he can tell: Michael must be on his rounds.

Seated out in his car, he lets the engine roar, then settle back to idle. No apprehension now. He takes the long curve of the Indian Ridge driveway slowly, then moves out into modest traffic. It is nearly dark. Car lights make driving easier, and he follows the bright red blurs of a truck back on to the thruway.

But what about Bea? He has neglected to tell Sarah the one thing she would have wanted to know, but never would have dared to ask—whether he stayed in love with Bea, too, all those years. He supposes he has, in a way. After all, he did try to look her up in a Seattle phone book once, then decided she wouldn't have stayed there after the war, and must have married. Or given him a made-up name in the first place. He knows there are ways now of searching for people by computers, and who would deny him that, at his stage in life, his wife in her condition?

The truck has taken the exit after the first abutment. The next is just over two miles away. He begins to accelerate, pulling into the fast lane. When tail lights grow bigger, he eases to the right, passing, then swerves back over to the left. He can't make out the needle on the dash but, no longer passed by anyone, he knows how fast he must be traveling. Fast enough the world has become a total blur. Bea and Sarah indistinguishable.

HARD COPY

So much is unknown. The big oak desk of course is known, the intercom angled on one side, monitor and keyboard, charts piled to her left and right, In and Out basket, papers strewn across the blotter and up against the faux-marble 2000 TEACHER OF THE YEAR pen holder. Known, too, her diplomas and certificates hung in pleasing symmetry on the wall, their protective glass reflecting the two arm chairs, the door ajar, the now black panes of her window. But what, at this after-hour, transpires beyond that dark geometry? What thrums in the hall beyond the door? What words wait on those papers? Unknown. It's all pretty much unknown.

Including the single sheet of paper pinned by her elbow to the desktop. As she works through the day's lab results—two days' really, what with the holiday and all—scribbling directions to Liz in the margins, referring to the charts as needed, checking her watch; the levering of her sunburned forearm, the riffling of pages, perhaps a slight draft from the air conditioning system, conspire to inch that paper closer to the edge. Then, before long, over the edge, until, its center of gravity finally reaching some critical point, it curves, slides free and rocks downward to land on the rug between her foot and the desk leg. A little farther and it would have landed in the wastebasket.

A little farther and who knows what would have followed?

It had to be Charles: she wasn't on call this evening.

"You up for the Thai place or you good with burgers again? Bunch left from yesterday."

"Burgers'd be fine."

"Randy ate already. So, fire 'em up?"

153

"Jesus, Charles. Call you when I'm leaving, okay?"

"Sure, hon. Sure. Sorry."

That set her back a few—the time, plus the time to regroup. PSA up from 3.6 to, what, 3.9 now. That matter in a year? Point 3? For a seventy-year-old prostate? To Sidney, yes—at his age everything, he says, matters. Lateral to urology—let them give him the finger.

Poor Charles. Doing his best. Just doesn't get it though. You take the 4th off and next day you've got twice the work. But it was worth it, even the sunburn, having everybody together—Melissa away from Nelson, Randy away from his shooter games. The lake had even made her forget about work for a few hours, forget about the residents starting July 1, managing her patients without a clue. Don't even know how to percuss anymore. Shouldn't have taken the damn day off.

PSA up → Uro

She underlined *Uro*, slapped the report onto the right-hand pile and grabbed the next one. Ten more minutes, she was out of there.

That was the thing about her husband: with nothing important in your life, trivia take over. Of course, he would say it wasn't burgers but writing that was important in his life. Which it was, to him, even if at age forty-seven he had nothing to show for it but an inch of magazines. Had to be. Can't live with yourself if you admit what you do every day doesn't matter. She was lucky that way. Everybody said medicine matttered. Why she went into it. Have to remember that next time she's pissed about staying later than the guys.

It was nearly eight when she carried the finished reports down the hall, tossed them on Liz's desk and continued on out through the waiting room. The noise she'd been vaguely aware of back in her office wasn't the air conditioner after all; it was a vacuum cleaner.

"Night!" she called across the big room.

The cleaning woman pulled her machine out from under a chair, straightened, turned, and smiled. In spite of the smile, though, in spite of her evident youth and her starched cleaning service uniform, she bore the weary look of her class. Dirt on her cheek. Dirt or a bruise.

Lucy wanted a cigarette in the worst way. Still had to get the groceries before they closed, though. She finished under the chairs, made a quick job of the rest of the rug, straightened *Time*, *People* on the last table. After storing the vacuum and cart in their closet, she noticed down the hall that the doctor had left her office light on. But when she got to the door, rather than reach in to the switch, she entered and picked up a paper lying on the floor by the waste basket. They weren't going to call her on that.

She sat down in the swivel chair, rocked back and forth, then, feet off the floor, gave herself a few spins. TEACHER OF THE YEAR she read as she leaned forward to pull the pen from its holder. Must be smart that doctor lady. Smart and rich. *But it is easier for a camel to go through the eye of a needle than for a rich man to enter the kingdom of God.* So reassuring and yet so troubling scripture, mixing grace and vindication.

Bread, Eggs, Salt, Beer, Cigs, Chips, Soup, she wrote on the back of the paper. Something else Lew wanted. Should have paid more attention when he said it. Not lottery ticket — always got that himself.

Folding the list twice she stood and walked out, hitting switches as she went. ARMED flashed on the keypad at the second try of her code and she was through the lobby and the big double doors with time to spare.

Outside it was still warm, the sky over the apartments glowing a pale lemon though it must be close to nine. She tipped a cigarette out of her pack, lit it, and took a long drag: with the Lord's help, this was her last pack.

The truck was half a block down the street. She'd been told not to park in the lots of the buildings where they cleaned: took up spaces the doctors and lawyers and their customers needed. She wouldn't have anyway, not an old Toyota pickup like Lew's, with a gun rack and that paint job of his.

Hot dogs! That was it. Or wieners, he called them. But she'd have to remember: nothing to write with now. As she

155

started the engine and pulled away from the curb, she kept repeating, Hot dog, Hot dog. She'd say it all the way to the store. There'd be the devil to pay if she walked into the trailer without those hot dogs.

Lew had the shade off the floor lamp and was holding the shotgun up close to the bulb. He'd checked it out the night he'd won it, but nobody'd bothered to tell him what to look for back then. Now, a year later, he knew—a guy on TV had a shotgun that looked just like his. Winchester Model 21. Custom. Worth ten grand, they said, maybe two, three times that at the right auction. You could tell by the fancywork, the serial number stamped....

The bulb was burning his cheek, but he didn't care: he could see there were some kind of marks on the chamber. Worn down, but could be numbers all right. He slid the shell in, snapped the chamber closed, and sank back into the couch. If only they'd do that show again, he thought, running the snowy channels: bastards talk too fast.

Light swept the room. A minute later the screen door screeched and there she came, ass-first, dragging the screen door shut after her.

"I know I'm late."

"See this?" He raised the gun from his lap but she kept right on into the kitchen. He stood to follow her.

"I said, you see this?"

A quick glance and she began taking cans from one of her bags, lining them up on the counter. "Yes, Lew, I see it. Your gun. Please don't point it like that."

"Sweet 16 they call this baby. Real sweet, too, if you wanna know—worth a shitload."

"I'm sure."

"Could be ten grand. More. Taking it in tomorrow before work. I'll need the truck."

She was more impressed with her bags, folding the empty ones and piling them by the trashcan at the end of the counter.

"Give me one of them," he said, as she moved toward the fridge with a 6-pack. She twisted a can free of its plastic ring

156

and handed it to him, a paper falling to the floor as she did so.

"Could we have the TV off?" she asked. "Or down? If you're not watching?"

"You don't care, do you? Don't give a shit."

"What?"

"'Bout my shotgun." He bent to pick up the paper. "What's this?" he asked. "Doctor love note?" He scanned it, both sides. "That what took you so long?"

Lucy took the paper from his hand, looked at it briefly, and gave it back. "My list. Couldn't forget your wieners."

"No wieners here. Doctor shit." Gun cradled in the crook of his arm, he balled the paper and tossed it toward the trashcan.

As Lucy finished with the groceries, Lew sipped his beer and watched her turn and bend and reach. When she went into the bedroom he followed her, beer in one fist, gun barrel in the other.

"Awful tired tonight, Lew. They had me on drapes all morning. Got to get some sleep."

She unbuttoned her uniform blouse, stepped out of the pants, and hung both on the hanger by the window.

"What?" she said as he watched her in her underwear tidying the bedclothes, then turning down the top sheet at an angle.

"You losin' interest? In your damn husband? 'Cause I'm onto somethin' here? 'Cause you might not have anybody to pray for no more?"

"Lew, what in the world...?"

"Or 'cause you're thinking 'bout the time I did? That it?"

"I know you did time, Lew."

"And you want me back there, don't you? You and your Jesus freaks. That's when you're interested. When I'm down. Drivin' shit cabs. Well, I'm not gonna be down no more, all right? This isn't the horses I'm talking about here, the seaweed. I'm past all that. I know where the smart money is now."

He shook the weapon at her, then tried to level it one-handed, but Lucy just got under the sheet and rolled toward

157

the wall. He leaned the gun against the wall behind him, drained the rest of his beer, crushed the can, and tossed it over his shoulder. Staring at the back of Lucy's head, he pulled off his T-shirt, undid his zipper and big buckle. The jeans dropped to the floor with a thud.

"You might be interested in my other gun," he said. He sat on the side of the bed, pulled off his shoes and then the pant legs one at a time with the socks.

"Lew," she whispered into the pillow. "Please."

With a flourish he jerked the sheet to the foot of the bed, grabbed her underpants, and dragged them the length of her legs.

"C'mon, Luce, you know you like it. Get that sweet ass of yours up here." He rolled her onto her stomach, hoisted her hips until she was on her knees, her back concave, her head between her elbows.

"Our father...." But her muttering didn't stop him. It used to, back when he first got out, when she still talked salvation and he felt there sure enough might be something there in the room with them. But not anymore. Nothing was ever there in the room with them anymore.

"Oh yes, oh yes," he began as he worked against her, thrusting to the rhythmic grate of the bed springs. Gradually his words turned into grunts, his grunts into cries, his cries into whimpers.

Slowly they unfolded, lengthening and flattening onto the bed as one. As he felt the rise and fall of the body beneath him, Lew welcomed the deep sense of satisfaction overcoming him.

It was a smart that woke him, making him cringe as he pulled away. Still dark out, and cool from the breeze through the trailer's open door and windows. Lucy slept, or pretended. He stood, ripped the sheet loose from the foot of the bed, and walked into the kitchen, wrapping himself as he went.

"Ow!" he muttered, a beer can skittering across the floor. Just one lousy 6-pack in the fridge. How long was that supposed to last him? He popped a can open, felt his way into the dark living room and collapsed onto the couch. No remote anywhere in the cushions. He pulled the light chain, took a drink, and blew out a long sigh.

At the end of the kitchen counter the silver cylinder of the trashcan reflected a shaft of light across the linoleum, across the balled-up paper. Cleans up after people all day, he thought, but won't even pick up the trash off her own damn floor.

He set the beer can down, tightened his cape around him, and walked back into the kitchen. He picked up the ball of paper, peeled back its crumpled folds, and smoothed it on the counter with the butt of his fist before heading back to the couch.

Yeah, doctor something. *RADIOLOGY ASSOCIATES*. They loved those big names, all right. Associates. *Ass*-ociates. Bunch of gibberish it looked like, too, filling the whole damn page. That's why they charge all that money. Fill up a page with shit nobody understands and tell you it's worth as much as an HDTV. Didn't say anything about the money, it didn't look like, but there was *IMPRESSION* down at the bottom. *Calcification...* whatever the hell that is *...and architectural* something, something *right breast highly suggestive of malignancy. Biopsy indicated.*

He crumpled the paper again and tossed it into the kitchen. "Bye-bye lady," he said as he groped further under the cushions for the remote. Finding nothing but a spoon and a corner of grit, he stopped, returned to the kitchen without his bed sheet this time and brought the paper back into good light.

Mary Longstreth it said toward the top. *12/09/1927.* Holy shit. So what's the big deal? Must be what the doctor figured. He was twenty-three. Where would he be at eighty? Wouldn't be in no fucking doctor's report, that was for sure.

"Hey Luce!" he called. "Lucy! Com'ere!"

When she didn't after a second shout, he marched into the bedroom and slapped the light switch on.

"I can't, Lew," Lucy whimpered as she swept her hand across the bed for the missing sheet. "I can't keep this up if you...."

"Where'd you get this?" He shook the paper at her curled, naked body.

159

"Get what?"

"This, for Christ sake! This... report thing. You steal it or what?"

"Steal it? Why would I steal it, Lew? It was in the waste basket."

"Doesn't sound like you neither, takin' shit out of waste baskets."

"Next to it I mean. It was on the floor next to the waste basket. Like it missed or something. She threw it and missed. I guess."

"She? This Mary whoever? Why would she...."

"No. The doctor. It's a she. Only one there."

"So you're telling me this she-doctor threw this away."

Lucy shrugged, rolled toward the wall.

"How come you throw something like this away?"

"Like what?"

"Jesus, Luce, you payin' attention? This medical report. How come you throw away a fucking medical report? Cancer and shit."

"*I* didn't throw it away."

She was dumber than he thought—Bible cloggin' up her brain. "Not *you*. If you're a *doctor* how come?"

"Maybe she didn't. Maybe it, I don't know, fell off or something."

"Off what?"

"Her desk. It was next to her desk. In her office. I'll take it back." She rolled toward him and beckoned. "Give it here I'll...."

"Oh no you don't." He jerked the paper away, picked up the shotgun still leaning against the wall. "Mine now. And you go tellin' anybody, I'll shove this barrel so far up you can spit buckshot."

Back on the couch he read more. *Rebecca Bouchard, M.D.* A woman—she was right about that much. Then lots of long words. But already he was worrying less about what exactly the words meant than how to keep them away from Lucy. Be just like her to try and get that paper back, now that he was interested. And it was her damn trailer: she knew every

160

inch of it. Could keep it in his truck but she'd snoop it out there, too. Say a prayer for where is it.

Naked, paper in hand, he paced back and forth, couch to kitchen, kitchen to couch. He'd think of something in his sleep—a lot of his best ideas came in his sleep—get it hidden once she'd gone off to work in the morning. Walking into the bedroom he noticed the gun still propped against the wall. He picked it up, fondled it, then peered down the bore.

"Lewis Fletcher," he muttered, "you are one smart son of a bitch."

Why had it always been easier to attend to the kids with their quarrels and their dioramas and their puberty, than it was to Charles? Well, not always. Not in the beginning, certainly, when a guy who talked about books and Big Questions rather than intermediary metabolism and cranial nerves seemed odd-ly—what do they say now?—hot.

Not much later than eight o'clock, but in spite of the high-test coffee, in spite of the pillows bolstering her on the couch, she could feel her lids begin to sag, her head jerk. Of course she was older, twenty years older than when the kids were kids. And it was Friday of a long week, made longer by those new residents, by the 4th, all that wind and sun and food at the lake.

She should be grateful, she knew, that Charles still talked, had something to talk about after spending another entire day in solitary. So many of her patients complained of having mutes for husbands. But that writing of his. Didn't he realize that now was not....

"And then how would Ibrahim get up to the intensive care unit?" he was saying, leaning forward in the easy chair, el-bows on knees, palms rubbing. "Can you just walk anywhere? In hospitals?"

"Pretty much. You could have him in a room at the end of a hall, say, near a stairwell, and he could go up or down. Course there would be security where the President was. Maybe the whole floor closed off, wing... Not sure how that works."

161

"In his gown thing?"

"Johnny. He could have brought clothes with him when he was admitted, or some uniform or something. You keep your suitcase in a closet in your room. 'Less you're in ICU. I showed you that time, remember?"

Charles pushed his glasses back up his nose, looked to the ceiling. "Security. Boy."

Plain old medical thriller wasn't enough for him now: had to be a terrorist in his hospital. An assassin. With gallstones— her contribution.

"Maybe if I shifted the point of view."

The ring of the phone caught her in mid-yawn. Charles looked at his watch, walked over to the desk at the corner of the den.

"For you," he mouthed, presenting the phone.

"Who?" But he only shrugged as she put the receiver to her ear.

"Doctor." The voice was rough, close.

"Yes? Who's this?"

"You missing anything?"

"Who *is* this?"

"Like one of your reports? Your doctor reports?"

She held the phone out; Charles returned it to its stand.

"What was that all about?" he said, sitting this time on the couch next to her.

"Some crank. Ought to give up the land line."

"Probably a wrong number. I always ask what number...."

"I know, Charles, I know. What you always ask."

But he did say, "doctor." And what kind of report? She let the phone ring three more times before she gave Charles the nod.

"So, you missing it or not I'm asking."

"Not that I know of."

"Well, according to what you don't know of," the voice went on, "this patient of yours here is going to die."

"What exactly are you talking about?"

"Jesus Christ! You a doctor or not? Tells what's wrong

162

right here on this paper I got, and I'm no doctor but sounds to me like somethin' better be done about it."

"All right, all right. Who's the patient? And what does it say?"

"Now we're talkin'. And you know what? You're going to find out."

She waited. Traffic, an argument, played in the background. She was hyper-awake now, keen to every noise as well as every silence, keen to Charles' looming curiosity as well.

"You still there?" she finally asked.

"Interested, huh? Pretty valuable information."

"Could be important."

A snicker. Or static. "Hundred and fifty grand valuable, matter of fact."

"What?"

"Hundred and fifty grand and it's all yours."

Again she held out the phone; again Charles took it back to the desk.

"Interesting," he said on his return.

She looked up at him, a tall man even foreshortened, chewing one earpiece of his glasses now. "I'm going to have to turn in, Charles, I think. Sorry but."

"Sure, Beck. Sure. Getting late. I'll close up."

As she lay in bed, her thoughts worked free of the call and around to Charles, his deference. What had always come across as passivity this time suggested something more willful, more comprehensive, like restraint. And she could tell he was still awake, probably as wide-awake as she with wondering, and all too aware she couldn't sleep. She hated to betray her state of mind, but the more she tried not to, the more she fidgeted, the more deeply she breathed.

Report. Not a word a guy like that used. Maybe he did have something. Unlike the men in her office, who'd been receiving their laboratory results on line for several years now, she still had hers mailed. What if your computer crashed, she argued, the intranet went down, power failed, as it certainly did from time to time in Maine? Viruses. Hackers. Paper was still best. She felt good about paper, about hard copy. Yes, about old-fashioned. Funny how she was becoming an old-fashioned girl after all. Went to Princeton in the first class to accept women, medical school as a minority, married a supportable man, kept her name, joined a medical group as their token female. And now, age fifty, she had to admit she found solace in some of the old-fashioned ways. Some of them.

"You all right, hon?" Charles whispered, as if Randy, three walls and an Xbox away, might hear.

"Yeah, fine. I'm fine. Sun did a job on my arms."

She felt his side of the mattress rise, heard the medicine cabinet open, water run.

Or just always let the machine take calls, she thought. Course then Charles would have heard the guy, if he left a message, and she'd never liked Charles getting involved with her work. Even office parties, tours of the hospital she took him on for his novel research. Something demeaning about it, to one of them at least.

Call made no sense. Like those lab results you dismissed because they didn't fit with anything else. Scam is what it was. Some guy trying to make a buck out of fear. Well, she wasn't in the fear market just then, never had been. Hadn't been afraid of a mother who told her baseball was for boys, a father who told her medicine was for men, professors who told her she was wasting their time, or partners who bet she'd choose kids over career and bail on them; and she for sure wasn't afraid of some jerk who thought any female picked out of a phonebook was a pussycat.

Charles was back, his breath in her hair, his hand on her shoulder. Wet fingers worked down over her breast as he pushed in close behind her.

"I want to help you get to sleep," he whispered. "Few more minutes—I just took a pill."

She rolled onto her back. Here came more work for her, with no guarantee of success either. But for this, too, she should be grateful: for a while at least she'd get that damn voice out of her ear.

164

Weekends, if Beck wasn't on call, Charles wrote early, before she got up, so he could be available when she did. And this Saturday, after such a hard week, he knew she'd be sleeping in, not as late as Randy, but nine maybe. It was still fairly cool, the ozone freshness of the air meaning an onshore breeze; and so pleasant looking out on the greens and textures of the woods, watching the finches and chickadees work the feeder. Needed to get more sunflower hearts, suet.

He sipped his coffee and went back over the section on gall bladder disease in Beck's textbook. Ibrahim had to convince the doctors—and the readers—of his symptoms, so he could get admitted and assassinate the President before the President had a chance to die on his own.

Little heavy on the irony. And gall stones? Should he really go with gall stones?

He closed the big volume and pushed back in his chair. Who did he think he was kidding? Ought to just go back to real estate. What he was doing when they met on Cape Cod. Writing, too, back then, but real estate was what you told people first, what he'd told her first back there on the beach. That was okay with her, it seemed, and the writing, too, when they got that far. The whole package must have been okay, even to this new doctor saving lives in Boston.

Yes, better to be good at what you *can* do, than bad at what you'd like to do. Be a role model for Randy, too, if a bit late. "Dad sits at a screen all day, why can't I? Dad does fantasy, why shouldn't I?" Why indeed? Freeloaders, both of them. Well, Williams in a month for his son, real estate license for himself, then Beck can relax, tell everybody her men are legit after all.

Crepes are what he'll make her for breakfast. Or take her out for brunch. Her money, his wallet.

Beyond the closed door he could hear the phone. Hear the pick-up before the machine. She was awake. Must be Melissa. Coming home again? Why didn't she just up and leave old man Nelson and,,,?

"You got the money?"

165

"Look, whoever you are, bug off. Next time I'm calling the police."

"Ooh. Police. And who you going to tell 'em's calling? Who this patient is? How bad off they are. And you know what?"

She wasn't answering, though she did want to know what.

"I'll tell you what. I hear from the cops and you'll never know nothin'. Leastwise till this patient of yours gets sick and I call 'em up and tell 'em what you should have known about 'em all along, and I tell some lawyers I know what you should have known about 'em all along and they die and it's your fault all 'cause of a measly hundred and fifty fuckin' grand that's chump change to you and a life to me.

"So, you got it or not?"

Beck pushed End and set the phone down on her bedside table. Just go through the records for the past, what, month? Six months? Year? He didn't say when it was from. But if the pathology was that serious, it wouldn't go back all that far. Have to check results in the computer against the paper ones in her charts, to be sure everything matched, that there was no paper report she'd somehow missed. For three thousand patients over a year's time. Plus consults. Plus Teaching Service patients, inpatient and outpatient records both. Could all be hired out, but who can you really trust? Would take nurses, at least, cost a lot, and not look so good. All these years she'd had to look better than the guys, and here all of a sudden she needs help with her records? Her vaunted paper records they still rolled their eyes at?

What's a hundred and fifty thousand dollars anyway? A slow year's take. Dip in the market wipes that out, and you don't bat an eye.

"You awake?" Charles was staring down at her.

"Half. Just lying here." She rearranged her pillow to gain a little height, a little control. "You been up long?"

"Hour or so. Crepes interest you? Got some raspberries yesterday."

"Sounds delish. Just give me a minute."

"No hurry. Oh, was that the phone just now? Not Melissa."

"No. This early? 'Nother wrong number."

She could feel him watching her as she swung her legs over the side of the bed. And as he left the room, the wake of his doubt as well.

Even though it was Sunday morning, and the office lot was empty, Lucy parked down the street. No one would know if she did park in the lot, but still. As she approached the office building, she could hear church bells, a sound that had always stirred her, even as a child before she'd found Jesus. She would have stopped if she weren't on a—yes—a mission.

The lock opened easily, security went to STANDBY the first time—good signs. Inside, she went directly to the file room where the charts were kept in floor-to-ceiling rows. She sat down at the narrow table by the wall, folded her hands, and bowed her head.

"Dear Lord," she whispered, "please give me guidance. Please also, Lord, allow me to remember the name. Mary—of course I can not forget that name—and L something, wasn't it? Please, Lord, I need your guidance. 'Let us walk honestly, as in the day.'"

She had prayed much like this just an hour before at the back of the Baptist church, and felt the spirit move within her, telling her to drive not back to the trailer, but into town and the office where she might, God willing, find the chart of the woman, Mary, whose report she had stolen. Yes, stolen, there was now no other word for it.

She started at the beginning of Dr. Bouchard's Ls, check-ing the first names. *Mary Ann Ledbetter*. Didn't look quite right, but in those few seconds, under that one kitchen light.... Opening the chart on the desk, she leafed through it until she came to what looked like test reports at the back. Chest X-ray from a year ago, mammogram.... She didn't even know what she was looking for. An absence. She turned back to the doc-tor's notes, abbreviated entries about complaints and drugs and more, but nothing about a missing report.

Hopeless. But would God have brought her here if there

167

was no hope? Or did He bring her here to prove to her that hope did not lie this way? Betraying your husband is not Godly: *Defraud ye not one the other.* So she had read that morning before church, Lew snoring naked on the bed as she scoured scripture for direction. *Let not the wife depart from her husband.*

The charts were wedged in tightly on their shelves. So hard to jam Ledbetter back in without tearing the cover; that, too, could be a sign: Ledbetter is the one, leave it out. Or—what are you doing here at all?

The doctor would have another copy of the report, in that computer on her desk, maybe; would in fact have meant to throw the paper into the waste basket because she no longer needed it. Had dealt with it. Whatever Lew meant to do with it would be, like so much he did, futile—the seaweed he was going to peddle to the mansions by the shore, the sulkies, that gun of his he was so proud of, then never mentioned again.

Oh, but if the doctor didn't know something important! If Mary didn't know.... What about the Samaritan—*Go, and do thou likewise?* Weren't those the Lord's very words, ringing now in her ears as Mary languished, helpless, perhaps, as the man on the road to Jericho?

Lew would be wanting the truck, an explanation for what took her so long. For the coffee and doughnuts, she would tell him. The fellowship.

She made her way back out of the office. If only he would consider coming with her one Sunday—one Sunday is all it would take. What it took for her.

It was hard to get through *JAMA*. Kook or not, that guy, she'd never liked being in the dark. Had spent her life, in fact, avoiding the dark, whether it was the dark of ignorance or the dark of her mother's decorum, her father's principles. She needed to talk to the guy face to face, man to man. As it were.

She put *JAMA* back on its stack. Next to the journals were the charts she'd brought home to dictate. Might have time while Charles did his *mis en place*, he called it, for Sunday dinner. Thank God he liked to cook. She never had, much less had the time—not since the days when her mother sat her on the counter in her little apron to measure out the cups and tablespoons, grease the pan, sprinkle the jimmies.

By the time she noticed the faraway ringing it was too late: she'd put the den phone on mute.

"For you," Charles said moments later, peering in around the door. "Patient named Smith? Should they be calling you on...?"

She picked up the receiver, waved him away.

"Got the meeting place."

She waited for the click of the kitchen phone. "What meeting place?"

"For the money."

"Blackmail is a crime. You know that?"

"I know killin' people is. And like I said, you go to the police, and that's what you'll be doin'."

"I don't even know you've got anything."

"Makes it interesting, doesn't it. But you're gonna know. You know the park, few blocks from your office? With the lake?"

She didn't answer: her silence was all she had right now.

"There's benches. Tomorrow nine o'clock you be sittin' on one."

Her mind was racing, a counterpoint of traffic and breaths in the background. By the lake they'd be out in the open; she'd see who he was, find out what he had. Name was all she needed.

"AM?" No answer. "And how'm I going to know you?"

But the phone was dead. Pay phone by the sound. He'd run out of change.

She picked up *JAMA*, against the chance of Charles walking in. She still wasn't ready to tell him anything, any more than she was her partners. Matter of fact, there was a lot now she wasn't ready to tell him. Over their twenty-four years, the imperative of confidentiality had crept far beyond its professional bounds. So far, in fact, that she couldn't imagine revealing—betraying was more like it—how she'd come to regard him: a well-meaning but ineffectual man whose original

169

charm she had found less original and less charming with each passing year. Writing was all well and good, but where was it going it hadn't gone by now? Wouldn't the response she'd get if she did confide in him be just another one of his scenarios? Wouldn't he go off on one of his tangents, one of his narratives that would leave her puzzled or annoyed or yawning? It would be like their sex. What she needed right now wasn't scenarios or narratives or sex; what she needed was counsel. The kind, unfortunately, she was the only one she trusted to give.

Smith? Same voice as before, and now he's Smith? "Got to speak to the doctor right away." Why in hell didn't she just hang up?

As his mind worked, he tidied the brightly colored piles on the cutting board—parsley, garlic, red pepper, onion. They were supposed to eat early, an old-fashioned Sunday afternoon dinner. Like he was going to be able to eat now. What was it with her? All that training, all that life and death, and she can't level with her own husband. Keeps talking to some jerk who calls her at home but....

He tore off his apron, strode down the hall to the den.

"Who the hell *was* that?"

"Shh! Randy." She frowned up at him, lowered the journal she was holding. "Patient. Got problems."

"Somebody does. How come he's calling you at home?"

"That's one of his problems. I'm about done here by the way."

"I bet you are."

"What's that supposed to mean?"

"Smith. Jesus, Beck, what do you want me to think?"

She stood. "Charles, that's the most ridiculous.... Guy's a mental case. If he calls again I'm calling the police. I told him that. And I will. Relax. Everything's fine. Go write your book."

A moment later she stood and reached up to kiss him on the lips. "I mean, need a hand in the kitchen?"

170

He would have whacked her one if she wasn't driving. The paper was his business now. She'd had her chance.

He pointed where to pull over, a shady stretch without meters a block shy of the park.

"You wait. Won't take me long. And when I come back, you and me, we're goin' to Vegas."

"I can't go out there, Lew. I...."

"You wait, you hear, or you'll damn well wish you had."

He got out and slammed the door. Get her away from that preacher, that's what he needed to do. Or, hell, she didn't want to go, screw it. Clean toilets the rest of her life.

Though it was only mid morning, the sun was high, the city heat muggy. As he'd hoped, not too many people were out, and moving through the park he saw it was mostly women with kids. At the lake, too, there was only some girl, it looked like, pushing a stroller, and on the far side a bag lady sorting her stuff. Not her, for sure.

He took his time once around the lake, glancing through the trees for any sign of the doctor, a lookout, police, then took a bench with a good view. Already a little after nine. They're always late, those doctors: first thing they teach 'em.

The stroller stopped across the way; the girl leaned down and picked up the kid. Cryin' its lungs out.

"Seat taken?"

He jumped at the sound. She'd snuck up on him from behind. Her all right, prettier than she'd sounded on the phone, with hair like on TV, and holding a canvas bag. Without an answer, she sat down, laying the bag on her lap. One of those grocery bags you buy. Something in it, too.

"Shopping?" he asked after a minute.

"Maybe."

"Lotta good bargains around, I hear."

"Like?"

"Oh, I don't know. Depends what you're after."

She turned to him now, for the first time. "I'm trying to help a patient of mine, actually. Someone's hurting him. Or her. I don't think he realizes the harm he's doing. This person, I mean."

171

"You must be a doctor then, you got a patient."

She turned away, pretending to watch the girl sitting now on a bench, bouncing the child on her knee.

"Well," he went on, "doctors can do a lot these days they say. Miracles and such. If they care enough about their patient. How about you? You care about your patient?"

"Obviously more than you do."

"Oh, gettin' into it now. But tell me this, would I have gone to all this trouble if I didn't care? Even *be* here? Just because I want somethin' for my trouble don't mean I don't care. You doctors want somethin' for your trouble, don't you? Last time I heard, the...."

"Of course something. Reasonable. I'm happy to pay you a reasonable fee, but what you said on the phone, which must have been...."

"Oh, I get it. This patient of yours might not be worth that much. That what you're sayin'? You're thinking about a what, twenty-dollar patient? Fifty maybe, if they're kinda like, movie stars or something? Well, looks to me like I put a little higher value on your patients than you do. And since I'm the one puttin' the value on, guess that's what it is. Let's see the money."

He pointed to the bag, which she only gripped more tightly, saying, "Let's see the report."

"What kind of a jerk you think I am? C'mon, lady."

He beckoned toward the bag and she reached in, pulling out... a newspaper. "You can't get that kind of money over a weekend. It'd take another couple of days. At least. If you could just in the mean...."

"Shoulda known. Drag me all the way out here and you got no money. My time's not valuable? That it? Well, my meter might just start tickin' again. But tell you what—give you one more day. Okay, make it Wednesday. Three o'clock. Here. After that, deal's off. You can just go about your pills and shit, wait for those lawyers to call, read that name in your damn paper. Then you'll find out. Everything. What you're gonna pay, how long you're in for...."

He stood and walked off before she could say anything

172

further. Doctors. Or is it women? Somebody, anyway, always making life so damn hard.

Beck's heart was still pounding from the run to her car. Smith, or whoever he was, had headed past the trees toward Filmore Street, it looked like. Scrawny guy, baggy pants, shirt out, dinky little goat beard—should be easy to spot, but nowhere along the edge of the park where she was driving could she see anybody. Side street did he take? Live nearby? Not this neighborhood by the looks. Then, just as she was about to turn, there he was, kicking a bottle along the sidewalk up ahead. She pulled in to the curb to let a van pass and watched as he went over to a parked pickup truck, looked around, opened the passenger door, and got in. Truck like that—gun rack, paint job—fit him to a Tee.

Barely a mile along the road, she could see the truck pull into a bus zone. A wait, and he got out, slammed the door, and crossed the sidewalk. The truck pulled out into traffic, someone's horn blaring, and was gone.

A&C Taxi it was where he went. Taking a cab somewhere? But you call cabs, you don't go to them. She waited fifteen minutes, but saw no cabs, no one else entering or leaving the building.

Back at the office she was late for her first patient. Liz went over the early calls, including Charles', and gave her the call-back list. She put on her white jacket and went into Room 2 with the first chart.

What old Ben Omeara was talking about, she couldn't figure out. Why Charles would be calling her she couldn't figure out either. What couldn't wait a few hours?

Maybe she wasn't up to figuring anything out that morning, except how A&C Taxi might help.

Twice while they did the dinner dishes Charles had asked Randy to take out his ear things. So they could talk, he'd said. Now that Randy had, Charles would have to actually say something.

173

"Hope you're not going to wear those during lectures."

"You read them on line, you know. Nobody goes to lectures anymore."

"Well, when you're reading them on line then. How do you think? All that noise."

"It's background, Dad. Everybody has background. It's one of our choices."

"Well, I just hope it's way background. We're not paying sixty thousand a year for background. Here, look at this—still sticky on the side."

He handed the rice pot back to his son. "So, your mother seem okay to you?"

"Wow. Nice segue, Dad." He made a show of scrubbing the pot with the sponge, then rinsed it and set it upside down on the drying rack. "Yeah, seems okay I guess. Don't see her that much anymore. Why? She doesn't to you?"

"I don't know. Something.... Ever say anything funny to you?"

"Mom? Funny?"

"Odd, then—out of character. You seem to pick up on stuff like that. I don't know, past few days...."

"Charles...." He turned and there she was, conjured by his efforts.

"I've got to go in for a little bit. Still haven't caught up from the 4th. And maybe I'll take the Passat. Needs to be driven. Won't be late."

"*That* odd?" Randy said, addressing the void his mother left. "I had the Passat yesterday. To the Mall. She knew that."

Charles pushed past his son and was in the Volvo before the garage door reached the floor. It took forever to rise, twanging the aerial as he backed out.

Still light: he'd need to keep a good block back. She seemed to be heading toward the office all right, but maybe she would at first, just in case. Driving fast, too, but then all of a sudden, for no reason, her brake lights lit, she was pulling over. To call Smith? Take his call? Always the safe driver even when you're.... No, not calling; getting out, turning, waving his way.

174

When he pulled up behind the Passat she came over to his window.

"Can't even tail people, can you? Write about it but...."

"Beck, I'm worried as hell. What in the world...?"

"Look, it's some crazy little...." She leaned into the door as if doing a pushup, then straightened. "Okay. This guy? Who's been calling? Name's Fletcher, not Smith. Prob'ly a kook, like I said, but says he's got some report. Some kind of patient report. I might have lost. And he's holding out, wants money for it, and I'm trying to deal with it. Didn't want to get you all... whatever, but I just... I just need to deal with it okay? Myself. Trust me, Charles. Please."

The look on her face had indeed turned plaintive. Alluring in a way he hadn't seen in a long time.

"'Course I trust you, Beck. But I'm coming."

"Charles, I can handle it. That's what I do. I handle things. Tough things. You'd...."

"I'd what? Screw up? Well, you're just going to have to take a chance on that."

"Jesus, Charles. Out of sight, then, okay? This guy, if he even suspects...."

He watched her walk along the shoulder to the car and get in. Staying well back he followed her through town and out through the suburbs to the next town over, a community of small farms interrupted here and there by grids of modular homes. Several miles out a two lane road he'd never been on before—Johnson Pike, a bullet-riddled sign said—she began to slow each time she passed a mailbox. Finally she came to a stop, backed up, then nosed through a break in a wire fence and disappeared beyond a stand of trees.

Charles pulled onto the shoulder, got out and ran to the opening. She had parked some hundred yards down a rutted track bordering a field, and was already out of the car, walking toward a solitary trailer that sat as if moored in a sea of weeds. No other vehicle in sight. She was carrying something, too—looked like one of his recycle bags from the garage. At the door she knocked, waited. She looked around, then back toward the road. Nothing was happening at the trailer. Thank

175

God—they could go home, have a little wine, finally get to the bottom of this. Could be a story.

He was starting down the track to meet her when she stepped away from the door and began moving along the front of the trailer, looking in the darkened windows. She disappeared around the far end and was gone a long time before reappearing. She stopped by a window, took something from her pocket and began working at the base of the screen.

With a screech the trailer door swung open. A man stepped out, naked but for boxer shorts. And a shotgun.

"What the fuck?"

"Oh! Sorry, I was just...."

"Just breaking into my house, huh? Laws about that, you know ."

"I do, I...."

"And you been followin' me. That's another one— stalking, I think they call it."

The barrel's black, dilated pupil stared her down. "No, no. I noticed, after the park, you go to the taxi place, and I just wanted to...."

"What? Just wanted to what? Get my name? Then go to the cops like I fucking told you not to? Jesus you make me want to ...."

"No, no, honestly I....."

The pupil kept staring but he was searching the field now, the woods, scowling toward the road. Slowly the gun barrel dipped. She breathed.

"Or give me something?" he went on. "Like what you got there this time? Couldn't wait till tomorrow? Let's have us a look."

He stepped back and motioned her through the doorway. It was dark inside except for a muted TV, a smoky den of a living room it looked like, kitchen at one end. The screen door slammed behind him.

"I couldn't wait to get this whole thing straightened out really," she began, surprised she could speak. "If somebody's sick I need to know about it. So I can help them. We all want

176

to help, don't we? And here's your chance to help, just as much as I do. More really. Wouldn't that make you feel good? And like I said, I'm happy to pay you. For calling, all this.... Anything really, I guess. Seeing as...."

"Happy. Yeah, happy. You look happy. You doctors always look happy, you know that? People dyin' all around and you're all happy. All set. Well, how about me havin' a turn? Give it here. Get that light."

He was pointing toward the kitchen. She flicked on the switch and returned to him, but didn't hand him the bag, not until he swung the barrel up again.

"Look, I'm sorry but I still couldn't.... why I came is to tell...."

"Feels pretty light, this bag," he interrupted, as he set it down on a chair and felt around inside with his free hand. "What the fuck is it with this bag?"

He dropped it and gripped the gun with both hands. Behind him, Charles' silhouette filled the screen door.

"Huh? You payin' attention? Steal my paper and put it in your fucking empty bag? That what you come here for? Well I...."

He wheeled at the screech, right into Charles' embrace. The gun clattered, as the two men crashed to the floor. Charles had it, Fletcher grabbing.

"Charl...!" she cried, buckled, blinded, by the explosion.

"Jesus, Jesus," Charles stammered in a drift of confetti. "Jesus Christ."

"Charles!"

And there on the floor, Fletcher twitched, oozing red from everywhere. Beck threw herself onto him—"Bleeding out! Your phone...."—and mashed the side of his neck, his bare, slippery chest. "Here! Pressure! Here!"

"No, Beck." He had her under the arms and was hauling her back. "Leave him."

"Gonna die on us!"

"Let him! Leave him be!"

"I've got to...."

"He *knows* us!"

177

She couldn't hold on, her hands so slick, her leverage so slight.

He was grunting, pulling her to a stand. "Get out of here before...."

"Wait! I've got to find...."

But he had her completely off the floor now, barging backwards out the door.

She'd never realized how powerful her husband was.

They were both there. Must be middle of the night, father fumbling with the light-chain, mother fingering her hair. Shiny. Wet. Odd.

"You awake, Randy?" she was saying. "Wake up. This is important. We have to tell you something. Can you take those things out of your ears? Please?"

"Ask you, really," his father corrected.

"There's been a terrible...."

"Let me, Beck," his father again, close. Not like him at all. None of this was like him. "Why we went out like that, your mother and I, was to pick up some papers from a... somebody about the practice that, well, that's not important."

He shaded his eyes, waiting till he could stand the light, stand the total oddness of it all—2:05 looked like the clock said, and were they going somewhere? Father doing the talking, about her practice. "*The* practice" he was calling it.

And now it's her again. "Anyway, he lives out of town, this person, and we drove out to his place...."

"In two cars?" He could think now, and had to ask. That many papers?

"Well, yes." His father shifted on the bed. "We'd both forgotten I'd said I'd go with her. But the point is, we got there and got out of the car—the *cars*—and just as we were walking in we heard gunshot. From inside the... the trailer. Where we were going. Or seemed like anyway."

They were studying him, his reaction, then it was his mother again. "You can imagine. A sound like that in the night. So we obviously turned right around and left. I mean."

Still watching, waiting. Was that *it*? Was he supposed to

say something now? Two in the morning you're supposed to ... what exactly?

"You see, Randy," his father went on, "thing is it might look kind of funny if someone thought we were around with, you know, guns going off."

"Not that anyone would have," his mother added. "Thought we were around, I mean. And we don't even know for sure it was a gun. Do we, Charles. Really."

His father considered for a beat. "No, that's right. Could have been a, I don't know, leftover from the 4th. But just to be on the safe side, why we woke you up, if anybody should ask you, or call, like the police or anybody, we'd just like for you to say we were here all evening. Like normal. Regular old normal evening. When your mother isn't on call. Which she wasn't."

"Sure. An alibi."

"Randy," his mother said, wringing his name the way she hadn't for years. "Don't put it like that. Makes it sound like."

"Okay. I'm cool with it. I guess."

"There you go." His father was trying to smile now, jiggling the bed slightly as he nodded. "Probably nobody'll call. Mountain out of a molehill."

"Thank you, Randy." His mother leaned over to kiss him on the forehead. "Sorry to put this on you."

"Hey, no prob. Sure I put plenty on you guys."

They didn't seem to be sure what he meant, maybe the tense of it. His father turned out the light and they left, pulling the door to behind them. He listened to their footsteps down the hall, the careful close of their own door. Probably talking in bed. About him. If he was still a kid, he'd do the keyhole thing.

But what it all came down to for him was, Do you owe your folks a lie? For giving you a life, maybe? And despite all they've counseled over the years? If so, do they owe you a truth? For giving them a son? Obligation ought to run both ways, oughtn't it? Three ways, actually—counting the one to yourself.

He put the buds back in his ears. Odd all right, even for a

179

dream.

In spite of Beck's pills, neither of them had slept. Periodically he hit a few keys in case Randy was passing by his door. He wasn't ready for the clarifications, the afterthoughts, daylight can bring. And everything would have to be coordinated with Beck. From then on.

No way he could concentrate on Ibrahim, though. Not with the world exploding every other minute, Fletcher flying backward, that face, blood. And Beck dripping red, struggling to stay when escape was all that mattered. But he'd done what he had to. He'd saved his wife. Killed a man — what does that mean, again, that *killed* he'd typed so many times? — but saved her. Good person for a lowlife: anybody'd go along with that.

Including Randy? Melissa? God, could they ever tell them? Pushes your capacity for trust, for shame, to the limit. Some day, maybe. Someday when he and Beck were lying side by side in their last beds and the kids were keeping vigils and the time was come when little mattered any more. There is one other thing, he'd say. One other thing you two should know.

The article in the paper was perfect: wife the prime suspect, abused and all. Motive, means. Nothing about any report. But how much did that wife know about it, how much might she be telling the police, the lawyers, right now? To deflect attention from herself. Or if she didn't know anything, the police might find the report themselves in the trailer, if they bothered to look. If there was a report. That was the thing: Beck kept saying she still didn't know there even was a report, a patient. After all that, a man dead, their two souls forever in thrall, they knew nothing for sure.

And like the part they'd told Randy, somebody could have heard the shot, the squeal of tires, could have caught one of their plates. Could be tire prints, too, in the track where Beck parked, on the shoulder where he did — thank God it was raining now. But finger prints — he knew about fingerprints, wrote about fingerprints, should have thought of fingerprints.

Okay, Ibrahim has a uniform in his suitcase in his room.

180

They don't check your suitcase when you're admitted, Beck said. Got it from... well, he'd work that out later when he could think. He takes off his gown, johnny, whatever, puts on the uniform and....

Have to be prepared. Be ready for the police. But they were smart, had that covered. Prominent doctor, respected, credible, just a parking ticket a few years back. Which she paid. Home all evening, both of them, she with her paperwork, taking care of patients on her own time, he watching TV. The night game. Grand slam in the seventh—you happen to see it, officer?

That whole night together, every variation considered. Except confession. Funny neither one of them mentioned confession. She must have thought of it, just as he had, but something like that you defer to the guilty one, the loved one. Be pretty easy, really: walk into the Scarborough police, ask to speak to the chief. That shooting last night? The trailer? Well, believe it or not it was me, but here's what happened.... Trial, jail maybe. Probably have a little table in your cell, pencil and paper. Might not be so bad. If that's how it went. Could be a long sentence, though. Life. Beck, too, if it came out she was—what do they call it?—an accessory. End of all her good. Bankrupt them, probably, with appeals. Kill her folks. Curse their children. All to the greater glory of the trailer people.

Blam!

If you don't believe us, officer, just ask our son. He's busy getting ready for college—Williams, by the way, maybe be a doctor like his mother—but he'll tell you. He was here. He'll vouch for us.

If they didn't believe her, they'd have to believe her supervisor. Her supervisor would say where she'd been: the doctors' office, cleaning, just like every Tuesday and Thursday for the past two years. And the keypad would say, too. Those things never forget.

Lucy ground out her cigarette and closed the Bible. *Valley of the shadow of death.* This was it, all right: the walls, the

181

lampshade ripped by death; the rug, all those little pieces stained the color of death. She'd get Resolve from work, a stiff brush. But what product would clean her, their "person of interest"? God's person of interest?

She couldn't stay another day in the valley of the shadow of death, the trailer of death. Stumble over that lump of Lew, riddled and sticky and still, every time she walked in. Behold that scowl every time she jerked up in bed. Terrible he was now, more than ever before, and so utterly beyond her saving. Beyond her loving, her ever having loved.

Our father who art in heaven. Thy will be done.

Couldn't leave, though. That was it: police told her that. Not until they'd checked everything out. And more than that, she couldn't go until she'd found the report. No luck in the night after the last officer and the ambulance and the reporters had left, after the first scrubbing and sweeping and prayers. That paper, that crumpled piece of paper no longer had the power of his salvation, but it did of hers. Sure as his murder was his punishment for abusing it, the scourge of his murder was her punishment for withholding the name, the holy name of Mary that meant more, she could see so clearly now, than any marriage vow.

Her knees burned against the bare bedroom floor. She raised her head and gazed upward.

Ceiling panels! She hadn't thought of ceiling panels; be just like Lew. Slowly she stood, then stepped up onto the bed. She pushed one of the rectangles aside and felt around the rough edges, tried the next one over as the springs grated beneath her. But a piece of paper! How was she ever going to find a single piece of paper in his world? He could have hidden it at the taxi office, in the truck, buried it in the field, the woods. He could have had it in his jeans all along, wadded up in a pocket with his tip sheets. The police had found his clothes and that recycle bag and taken them with them, would find the paper, check with Dr. Bouchard, get the information where it belonged, leaving her to live and die and burn with private failure.

"You weren't on call last night were you?" So damn sharp, that Liz. Should have known she'd pick up on something.

"No, do I look it? Hot flashes. We still have any of those estrogen samples?"

That was true, though, in the new way of truth—hot flashes. Waves of sweat and panic as they whispered and waited in each others' arms for the ringing of the phone, the pounding on the door. But nothing had happened, thanks, no doubt, to their talk with Randy, their preparation for the worst.

And then at last the sky had lightened, the birds had begun on the feeder, the paper had hit the porch as if just another day were starting. And there it was, its own little paragraph in *Local*, the kind of news she'd never stooped to read before. Murder. Abuse. Nowhere in those words did they find themselves, nowhere in that godforsaken trailer. How could they have? They were at home all evening. They and their son were at home the entire evening. They were normal.

But the bag. The damn recycle bag that might have a receipt. How could she have left it? How could she ever have thought it would fool him?

And the wife. Widow and suspect in one. Too bad, that's all. You make a life like theirs, and things like that happen. Hadn't she tried to stop the blood? Tried to call for help? Hadn't Charles stopped her, doing what he thought best? Was he obliged to step forward? Was she obliged to sacrifice him, not to mention herself, and for what?

For a patient? For that mere possibility of a patient out there? How fortunate merely to be ill, merely to be mortal, merely to be ignorant and innocent. A malpractice suit had never looked so good to her before, even losing it a relative win, compared to....

Win. Win some, lose some—her resident's mantra back in Boston. Beck, he'd say, wiping the electrode jelly off the quiet, singed chest, way you've got to think about this one if you hope to think about the next one. And she did learn that about winning and losing, about staying sane and normal for the next life to save.

183

Normal she was, though what exactly *is* normal, when you've got that ringing in the ears, that image of agony and snowfall etched in the eyes? Maybe she didn't know anymore, though Liz did, and now was back, leaning in the office door.

"Sorry to bother you but just heard one of the cleaning women—who does us? after hours?—lost her husband last night. Card? Flowers? Might be good PR."

"Sure. Fine by me. Run it by the guys, though." And then she added, struggling to be normal, "Not one of our patients, I hope."

"No, no. I checked. Some guy in a trailer. Shot or something."

She swiveled back to her desk, papers scattering.

Her. Fifth it was, night after the holiday. With the bruise. Knew everything, then—the calls, the park, the money.

She grabbed her cell. Ringing on top of ringing.

"Hello?"

"Charles!" almost strangling on her whisper. "The wife! Works here. She...."

"God, Beck, I thought you were the cops."

"...She stole it. Knows all about it. Going to blackmail us herself."

"Can hardly hear you, Beck. Speak up, can you?"

"She'll tell the police about me unless I... I don't know... say I saw her here last night. Want the money, too, for the report, her silence. Maybe lots. She's got us, Charles. She's got us."

"Give her the damn money. But you can't have been there, Beck. Randy—remember?"

Flashing—the intercom.

"Not now, Liz."

"She's on six."

"Who?"

"The widow. On a pay phone. Put her through?"

184